D1525354

# The Price of Faith

Rebecca Cooper

**Notice of Copyright**



FIRST EDITION

www.rebeccacooperauthor.com

**Printed by:**
Amazon Publishing

Printed in the United States of America
**First Printing Edition, 2021**
ISBN 9798781410279

This is for the ones that show up for love over and over again – even when their hearts are broken. Even when it's hard. Even when they don't know how they'll ever make it through.

This is for the ones that still say *yes*.

**Table of Contents**

*Grief is the price that we pay in order to know that we have loved.*

## The Beginning

**Beginning: The point in time or space in which something starts**

**This is it. This is the beginning.**

I still went to work.

"They" said to take the money anonymously.

So I did.

I kept it a secret from every single person that I knew and loved.

$1.2 billion.

Even saying it is heavy. Like the words clang around my mouth and my tongue kind of stumbles.

Billion.

It was the largest lottery ever won by anyone in the history of all time ever. And it all came to me. I was the only winner. All of it.

Some money was, of course, lost to taxes, but I can't tell you how much and that, of course, is not the point of this particular story.

Largest lottery ever.

The country was in a frenzy. Who had won? Grandpa? Your neighbor?

Or me. Just an average girl in literally every single sense of the word.

The girl with credit card debt and a passion for Hobby Lobby and beer. The girl with a kind of boyfriend and a kind of pet cat that only visited when they wanted food or attention. I had a normal job as a nurse on the general surgery floor, and I always drank too much coffee.

One day, I was contemplating a balance transfer on a credit card and stealing the wifi at McDonald's (right behind my shitty apartment), and the next? I had over a billion dollars in my checking account.

You guys. Before this money? I didn't even have a savings account.

The lottery guy with the kind eyes and whose name I don't remember smiled at me and said, "Well, I guess this sort of changes things."

Yeah. You could say that again.

And again.

And again.

## Lesson #1

**Anonymous: Not identified by name; of unknown name**

**The lottery winner was *anonymous* until she just ... wasn't.**

I still went to work.

The country lottery sleuths had narrowed the winning ticket to a small Kwik Shop down by the hospital. Speculation was rampant. Was it a deserving patient? Someone who can now afford that heart surgery? A custodian? The lady that serves the warm chocolate pudding on Thursdays?

Maybe it was a doctor, and since he or she is probably already wealthy, maybe he or she will donate it back to the city.

In my head, I screamed back at the TV. Nooooo! Just a nurse that made out with her biology professor to make it through nursing school. Just a girl with a fake Coach bag that she's pretty sure she bought illegally.

What I really mean to say here is that I had $1.2 billion and I couldn't tell anyone. Or that's how I felt. Not even my parents. *Not even my parents knew.* And I actually *like* them.

On a day off, I met with a man named Marshall. I wore my favorite ripped jeans that hadn't been washed in a couple of ... weeks ... almost in some sort of act of defiance. The lottery guy with the kind eyes hooked me up with him, and I was so grateful for some sort of direction. Marshall was a financial planner that would become a godsend to me. Quiet, smart, and a dry sense of humor. My kinda people. He did a bunch of Marshall Magic, and suddenly, I had a savings account, and a monthly budget. My debt was paid off. And the small debt that my parents carried was set to be paid off ... which kinda meant that I was going to have to tell them. Eventually.

Suddenly? A check was deposited into that brand new checking account of mine on the first of the month. *One hundred thousand dollars* would just magically appear every single month for the rest of my life.

Marshall determined that I'd meet with him on the first of the month - every month - to discuss my spending and my portfolio. Because I had one now. Apparently, the crew at the lottery commission took pity on the young girl with all. the. money., and were prepared to not let her fail *spectacularly*. Marshall was to "counsel" me about investing and stocks and just ... *money* stuff. He would become one of my financial lifelines.

The first month that the money appeared in my checking account, I splurged on coffee. I bought groceries at the expensive grocery store and not the Wal-Mart. I managed to dip into my account - the one with the lottery money - twice. Of the shiny new ONE HUNDRED GRAND, I only spent $600.

Marshall just smirked at me. "Are you scared or something?"

I blinked back at him. *Yeah.*

On the way home, I downloaded a home buying app, because #millennial, and spent the next four days agonizing over granite, or concrete, or quartz, and what 25-year-old needs a marble countertop?

On Day 5, I deleted the app.

On Day 6, I opened my computer and started searching for a new apartment. Stainless appliances in the heart of the city. A built in gym that I'd never use. These kinds of things I could handle. This was the kind of thing I could live in.

I called Marshall.

"Maybe you won't have to steal wifi anymore," he chided me. "I'll get you out of your lease." See? *Marshall Magic*.

I called the listing agent and set up a moving date. It was all so much easier than I'd ever imagined. Turns out, money really helps.

I looked around my apartment. Handed down bed from my mom's friend. Headboard from the side of the street. Dressers from when I was five and a coffee table from the Goodwill.

$100,000 on the first of every month and I was sitting on a couch that still smelled sort of like the bad decisions I made in college.

I called the local thrift stores and for a nominal fee - they sure do come and haul stuff away. I realized, perhaps for the hundredth time just that day, things were going to be upside down. Fantastically different. I was stepping into a world I'd never known.

Somewhere in the span of these six days, I realized that I'd need to inform my parents. And I know what you're thinking. I *know*. Why didn't I tell them to begin with, right? They must be crazy, or awful, or evil. Right?

Wrong.

My mom is a pediatric nurse in the same hospital as me. We eat lunch together nearly every time we're at work. My dad is an engineer. Or was. He was retired. "And with good financial planning," he always tells me, "you, too, can retire early."

Yeah. Okay, dad. He might actually die of a heart attack when I tell him. Maybe that's why I've put it off. I'm *actually* scared for their well-being.

I eat lunch with them every Sunday after church. I'm an only child, and I love my parents. My mom is my best friend and my dad is my hero. This is the first thing I've hidden from them, since ... well. That's not important.

The trouble here is that I can hardly believe any of this myself. Can hardly make heads or tails of it, let alone, like actually *speak* about it. I kept thinking I'd wait until Sunday lunch. And then a month passed. Four Sundays. And then another month. Eight.

And here we are. I'm a 25-year-old billionaire, and all the while, my dad is certain that the next thing out of my mouth is going to be a request for money for my car payment.

Again.

The Sunday before I was supposed to move into my shiny new apartment, I decided that it was time. They'd surely realize that something was up when they came to visit and they ate off of new plates and sat on a new couch at a whole new apartment that was *definitely* out of my normal price range.

It was time.

Mom made a spaghetti bake for lunch. I don't remember tasting it. I don't really remember much of anything until I heard my dad's fork hit the plate.

"Dammit, Grace."

It was his dad voice and I was certain that I hadn't done anything to deserve THAT. My head shot up. "What?" I wiped my mouth.

My mother's eyes were trained on mine and they were worried.

"What the hell is wrong with you lately?" His face looked hard and angry.

"What?" I stuttered. Again.

"Weeks now. Weeks. You've been ..." He trailed off.

My mother, Caroline, filled in, as she often does. "Absent."

"Yes," he continued. "Absent." He cleared his throat. "Now. Whatever trouble you're in, we can help you. You just have to tell us."

My mom's stare was unnerving. *Trouble?* I winced at the words.

"Is it drugs?" Mom's voice was deathly quiet. "Are you stealing them from the hospital?"

Those words *actually* came out at the same time my dad offered to pay whatever bill I needed.

Whatever I needed from them.

They were going to die. They'd rescued me a thousand times. And I was the girl that was *always* in the thick of it. Together, they'd pulled me out of so many bad spots, and now here I was ... about to tell them that for once? I was the lucky one.

"What is it, Grace?" My dad again. Much more concerned this time. His voice had softened and his hand was on mine from across the table.

"Grace?" My mom. She was going to shit her pants.

I put my fork down and looked at them both. Mom. Dad. Then mom again. Mom's eyes would be easier to look into. I stuck with her.

I cleared my throat. And then again. "You know the 'Cincinnati Billionaire' thing?" I named the ongoing news story about the biggest mystery in our town's history.

Oh, mom. She looked so confused. And then? The light went off.

"You know who won? Who is it? Are you dating him? Is that what this is about? Oh!" She abruptly stood and squeezed me in a Momma Bear Hug.

"No," I said a little too forcefully. "No." I gently pushed her away. She stood awkwardly next to me.

"Then what?" Dad was now calm. His voice was calm mixed with ... what was it? "Grace?" Yes. There it was. *Trepidation*. Still certain he was going to have to bail me out. (To be fair, he's had to bail me out too many times.)

"Me." I looked at him. I was wrong. Dad was easier to look at. "It was me. I won."

Silence descended.

I was anonymous no more.

Mom plopped back into her chair and my dad stared at me slack-jawed. I can never stand silence like that, so I continued, vomiting a riot of words from my mouth. Words I'd kept locked away for two months now.

"They advised me to stay quiet for a while. Until I figured it all out. Advised me to not even tell my family. They assigned me a financial planner, Marshall."

Truthfully, that's as far as I'd gotten in my head ... I had expected -

"WHAT?"

More questions.

"Marshall?" My mom's delicate voice. The one she uses on sick kids.

"Is this some kind of joke?" Angry dad made another appearance.

"No, dad. It isn't." Disbelief. *That* I recognized. "His name is Marshall Graves, and he's been managing my portfolio."

"*Portfolio*?" My mother stared at me like I was some kind of zombie. This was the woman that used to shove twenties in my laundry basket. This was the woman that still took me shopping for new clothes.

"Yes." I shuffled my feet. "I'm sorry I haven't told you, but I hardly believe it myself."

My dad cleared his throat. "Start from the beginning, Grace." Ah, *this* dad. This is the one that I could talk to. Make sense of things with. This was Logic Dad. We were finally getting somewhere.

So I did. I started at the beginning.

...

I drove my beat up Camry to the Kwik Shop by the hospital. I was almost late to work, but I needed coffee. Lots and lots of coffee.

Lawson had invited me over to "talk" the night before, and really, that just meant regrettable, forgettable sex. And now, I was just ... *tired*. Of him. Of the constant feeling of knowing I deserve more. Of his awful bed.

So. Coffee. Kwik Shop.

The lady at the register - the now $50,000 richer Susannah - offered me a lottery ticket.

"Over one billion dollars," she said - her bubbly excitement flowing into my parched, tired brain. Her purple fingernails tapping on the cash register keys, and the gum between her teeth snapping with each popped bubble.

"Better give me two, then," I smiled back at her. She was always there. She was always so happy.

Tickets in hand, I headed to work. I didn't check my tickets for two days ... not until I saw Susannah on the front page of the paper talking about the "Cincinnati Surprise". I pulled my now rumpled tickets out of my purse and literally stared at my computer for three hours.

That's when I read the back of the ticket.

That's when I signed it and shoved it into my bra.

That's when I called in sick to work the next day.

That's when I lost my damn mind so hard that I even cleaned out the inside of the dishwasher. Did you know there was a filter in your dishwasher? I didn't until that night.

That's when I panicked because I thought I'd sweated through the lottery ticket paper - still stuck to my boob in my bra.

...

My dad cleared his throat and pulled me out of my revelry. "You cleaned out your dishwasher?" He was incredulous. I was, too. I get neurotic when I get nervous. What can I say?

"Yeah." I shrugged my shoulders.

"And you didn't call us?" My mom was hurt. I could see it through her disbelief.

"I didn't believe it myself. Not for a second. I thought for sure that I'd walk into that office and they'd laugh at me. No sense in getting you worked up if that was just going to happen, I guess. And honestly? Telling you? That'd make it all real. And real? Real is ... scary. For me, anyway. Really scary. I mean, what do I do with A BILLION DOLLARS?"

Neither of them spoke. Presumably because neither parent knew. For once, I'd stumped them.

"Well," my mom said, finally sitting back in her chair. "At least you don't have to work under that damn Dr. Heatherton anymore if you don't want to."

My head jerked to her. Dr. Heatherton. The love of my life. The man who didn't even know I was alive, and the man my mother swears to loathe for the rest of ever. But his ass. In scrubs. *Lord have mercy.*

I sighed. "I can't ... I can't not work." Oh, I'd thought about quitting. Yes. But then when would I ever see Dr. Heatherton? Never. Or. Unless I needed my appendix out. Which I don't because it came out in the third grade.

Dad looked to mom. "I should call Sean."

Sean. Our family attorney. Card carrying member of the Good Ol' Boys Club and my godfather. A brick that I hadn't realized was in my stomach disappeared. Relief washed over me. I should've told my parents weeks ago.

They must've seen it in my face because mom wrapped her cool fingers around mine and dad got up to call his oldest friend. My dinner still sat in front of me.

My mother suddenly squealed in front of me and squeezed my hand oh-so-hard. "You can pay off your student loans!" she yelled.

And I laughed. That was the first thing I listed when Marshall asked me about debt. Student loans. "And your house will be paid off, too," I added quietly. Her eyes filled with tears. I could hear my dad on the phone.

*Right away.*

*Emergency.*

*Now.*

Poor Sean. He was going to get here and think someone was dying.

And I was right.

He burst through the door like a pit bull - all 6'8" of him.

"What the hell is the matter, Morgan?" My dad's name was actually Randolph Morgan, but everyone affectionately referred to him as Morgan.

His eyes must've fallen on me and mom sitting at the table, with mom's eyes still all weepy from the house thing. "Grace? Honey? What's the matter?"

Sean. Sean had fixed everything for me nearly ten years ago and ever since, he's guarded me like the damn bear he really is.

"Grace?" My mother prompted me.

I looked up at Sean's clearly distraught warm, brown eyes. "I won the lottery."

A loud laugh - one befitting a three hundred pound man fell into the quiet space. "You called me out of a golf outing with the mayor for some kind of joke, Randolph?"

Well, now he was pissed. That first name really drove that point home.

"I'm not kidding." I stared at him, willing him to believe me.

In the end? It took me pulling up my banking app on my phone while he had one hand on the door ready to leave. The zeroes were astonishing to the crowd around me.

"Jesus, Grace." Sean stared at me.

"I know." I shrugged.

He sat heavily in the chair.

"What do we do, Sean?" My mom's voice called from the liquor cabinet. She was making a gin and tonic for dad and Sean and a Manhattan for herself. I'd seen her do it a thousand times. I didn't even need to look. Instead, I stared at the wallpaper border I helped her hang almost ten years ago.

The summer that Sean saved me. It was gingham, and lining up those lines was a bitch. That's probably why it was still hanging in the living room.

"I don't ..." He sighed from the chair. "Let me think for a second. This is the last thing I expected to hear. Just ... let me think for a second."

My mom handed him a drink and he drained it in one swallow. "You were the sole winner, right? I saw that on the news. Only one winner." He looked at me.

"Yep." My eyes didn't stray from the pattern in the wallpaper.

Seconds ticked by. My mother's ice clinked together, as she, too, drained her glass.

Sean suddenly leapt to his feet. I swear I felt the house rumble. "Okay." He stared at the table and I knew a plan was coming.

"What I do know is that money changes people. And never for the good. You'll need a team, Grace. A team of people with your best interest at heart. And ... you need to keep it quiet. A billion dollars could persuade *anyone* to do something stupid. I'll, uh," he wiped his now sweating forehead with a handkerchief from his back pocket. "I'll draw up some non-disclosure agreements for friends or whatnot. And paperwork for a will."

"A will?" My dad cut him off. "Nobody is dying, Sean. Don't be dramatic."

"That's what I'd tell Trisha." Trisha. His own daughter. "You just never know. She needs to be as explicit as possible. And for shit's sake, Grace, move out of that piece of shit apartment and into something with a doorman or better security."

I just nodded my head.

"Other than that, I'm not sure, Morgan. I -- I'm just not sure." My dad and his oldest friend each nodded at each other. "A billion dollars," he mused.

"I know. I knooooow." I was still baffled by it all myself.

Sunday lunch ended much like it always did. Mom kissed my cheek. Dad hugged me. Sean stood by, probably waiting to walk me to my car.

"Of all the things, Gracie," mom's voice trailed off. "Of all the things I thought you were going to say - it was certainly never this."

I just nodded. The lump in my throat kept me from saying anything else.

For some reason, standing in that foyer ... my old foyer ... for some reason, I felt an ending happen. I felt a book closing, perhaps. I was no longer a burden to my parents. No longer was I a girl they had to clean up after. No longer Gracie Morgan: The Girl That Had 'The Thing' 10 Years Ago. No longer their mess.

Sean chuckled suddenly. "I bet work is a lot more fun now that you can leave whenever you want."

Sean.

Always ready with a joke.

"We'll see you guys later." He opened the door for me and ushered me out. By my car, he paused my hand on the door. "I'm serious, Grace. Keep it quiet until we can get a hold on things. People turn stupid when money gets involved."

I could only nod again. The lump in my throat still hadn't dislodged. I felt like I had arrived as a kid and now I was leaving - as an adult. It didn't feel real.

## Lesson #2

**Work: Activity involving mental or physical effort done in order to achieve a purpose or result**

**Romance: a feeling of excitement and mystery associated with love**

**The pair began an unlikely work romance.**

Lawson was unsurprisingly easy to blow off. My girl heart knew it was about sex anyway, and my clitoris wasn't sad to see him go. Neither was my g-spot, which he couldn't find with a map AND Siri helping.

I digress. Lawson was out. And I started bringing baked goods to work. Because I could afford to grocery shop for whatever I wanted. That included the good chocolate, apparently. Twenty dollars every few days and it would only take six million years to get through all of my new fortune.

Lawson was gone and mom emailed me a link an hour to a couch or a recliner or a platter or a Louis Vuitton tote. I basically spent my days staring wide-eyed at the people around me.

Starting IVs.

Administering medication.

Cleaning up two a.m. puke.

Charting blood pressures.

Chanting *billionaire* over and over again in my head.

Volunteering for all of Dr. Heatherton's surgeries.

Ordering *actual* coffee at Starbucks and skipping Susannah and the shitty gas station coffee.

At the nurses' station one night, the good doctor himself stopped by. "Are you okay, Grace?" His voice was soft and the quiet, dark hour made it seem much more intimate than it probably was.

I stopped charting. "Yeah? What do you mean? Of course I'm okay." *Not.*

He sucked in his lower lip and I kinda lost a little focus.

"You've been distracted lately." He toyed with a car dealership pen. (The very best kind, in my opinion.)

"I ..." I stuttered. Typical around him. "I'm sorry. I'll do better."

He smirked. "There is no better, Grace. I just hope that whatever is bothering you ..." He trailed off. Definitely *not* typical for him. "Resolves itself. Soon." He sort of smiled in a trademarked, pained kind of way, and then walked away. I was left panting like I'd run a marathon or something equally as stupid.

And ... did he just? Did he just *compliment* me?

What the hell was even going on in the world? I mean I did those stupid wealth and life affirmations sometimes that I watched on TikTok, but I'm really pretty sure they're not supposed to work *this well.*

I shook it off. Cleared my head. No time right now to really be distracted by a man in perfectly fitted scrubs.

But for real. *The scrubs.*

My "friends", as I'm sure you're wondering, have sort of been lost in the fray. After school, we kind of all went our own way. And it wasn't exactly like I was ever super friendly, anyway. I'm still in that "finding my own way" place and the rest are married, baby-making factories. Conversation with them always centers around things I don't really know about and laughing in the places where they pause for me to. And if you knew me? Like really *knew* me? You'd know that I have walls about ten feet high all around me - *for good reason.* My friendships were surface deep - *on purpose.*

To not have mentioned my billion dollars to these "friends" ... to not have mentioned Dr. Heatherton to them ... neither one seemed weird to me. Okay. It's crappy. Still. I know. But in my defense, what do you even say?

You know what? That's why Heatherton sees me distracted every day.

BECAUSE I AM.

...

Over the next week, Heatherton stopped to compliment me two more times. The second time, I just stared at him like he had lost his damn mind.

"What's wrong with you?" I side-eyed the hell out of him.

His chart nearly fell to the desk. "What?"

I smiled at him. A billion dollars makes a girl brave, I suppose. "What's *wrong* with you?" I said again - much more slowly.

"I mean ... Nothing? What's wrong with *you*?" He looked down at his chest like I had asked him about some sort of physical impairment.

"I didn't even know you knew my name until a week ago." I raised an eyebrow.

His phone sounded an alarm. He was literally saved by the bell. He smiled a very rare full-wattage smile at me. "I've always known your name, Grace." He picked up his abused chart and walked away.

And color me surprised. I stared at him - AGAIN - as he walked away. For two years now, I'd worked on the general surgery floor. For two years, I've watched him.

Okay. OKAY. Fine.

For two years, I've secretly been in love with him. Like hardcore love. Like the kinda love you feel in second grade it's still all pure and true and you make cut out hearts for them. That kind of love.

Do you know if he dates anyone?

I don't either.

Married?

Don't know.

Doesn't wear a ring.

I've been too terrified to ask, too.

Because Heatherton doesn't have the best reputation. Even my mom hates him and she loves everyone. No one really knows why, either. I asked about a dozen times my first year. Bunch of shoulder shrugs and non-committal grunts. He's good - *very* good at what he does - and part of me feels like the dislike is based in the envy of his finesse.

Whatever.

Anyway.

Pretty sure he was hitting on me.

And pretty sure I was going to be okay with it. He could do it again and I totally wouldn't mind. I glanced back down at my own chart, willing myself to focus again. Willing myself to settle down.

"He likes you," Tabitha's voice jarred me again. I shut my chart.

"Doubt it," I turned and smiled at her.

Tabitha was my mom's age and mothered every person on this floor. "No," she continued. "He does. I can tell. And it hasn't happened here *ever*." She gave me a look that spoke ALL of the volumes. She *knew* something.

"You know his story, don't you?" My eyes widened. "Holy shit! Spill it!"

"Not my story to tell." Cryptic. Tabitha was all cryptic.

"Give me a hint, then." I waved my hand around in the air. "Something." I sighed. "Everyone hates him. Should I? Is this stupid?"

She contemplated a second. "Ever think that he's not the life of the party around here for a reason? Maybe people don't like him because he's never at the mixers, never opens up, never ... brings his personal life to work?"

Of course I had. Because I love him. I noticed everything.

"He was married once." She said, looking at the wall over my head.

Except that. I didn't know that.

"And now? He's not ..." She turned back around. "Just keep that in mind." And our conversation was effectively over.

*Interesting.*

I had the next two days off for moving purposes.

And furniture purposes.

And I bought a new purse and I left the box it came in on the floor in my closet. My closet that was mostly … empty. What pitiful wardrobe I had only took up a small corner of the walk-in.

My new house smelled like a showroom and my parents and I stood there after the movers left in some kind of rare silent awe. The pretty, heavy white dishes. The gorgeous silk curtains. And a duvet. I owned matching bedding. Which is where my new Louis Vuitton bag was currently resting. I was terrified to touch it.

"This is the strangest thing that has ever happened to me," I supplied unnecessarily. I looked at my new lamps. They matched.

Years later, I'm positive that I'd still have those $200 Pottery Barn lamps because *expensive*. I almost choked at the counter when I paid for them.

"We should stop somewhere next weekend and work on your wardrobe." My mom giggled as she spoke.

"And we should figure out a ... *cause*," dad called to me as he plopped onto my new couch. "This is pretty nice." His hands petted the material.

We all followed him to the sectional. I'd paid off all of their remaining debt. The rest of their house. Mom's car. I had nothing else to spend money on. Dad was right. I needed something to give some of my resources to. Something to make an impact.

My cell rang as I contemplated. My new cell phone. An upgrade. Because that's what Sean suggested when he called for the thirtieth time that week about security measures.

"Hello," I called. It was a hospital extension. They'd called before when they needed extra help. Looked like my couple of days off were about to be cut short.

"Grace?" Nope. It was just Elijah Heatherton. On my new phone.

I cleared my throat. "Dr. Heatherton?" I turned quickly away from my mother's widened eyes.

"Is this a bad time?" I could hear the smile playing on his lips.

"Uh. Well ... No? Is everything okay at the hospital?" I fiddled with a new dishrag from William Sonoma.

"Yea. Everything is fine here. I - I just ..."

"Yes?" What. The ever. Loving. Fuck.

"I was just wondering if you wanted to meet me for a drink tonight ... Or ... whenever you have a second."

I stared at my stainless steel oven. What? "To talk about work ...?" I had to be sure.

"If that's what you'd like to talk about. I was thinking it could be ... a ... *date*." I could almost hear him bracing himself.

A date? With the *actual* man of my dreams?

I'm living in an alternative world. Pretty sure this is the Matrix or something.

A billion dollars.

A new apartment.

A new boy?

I looked up at the ceiling praising whatever God decided to show me all of the good fortune.

"Uh? Grace?" His voice was tight. Pained. Like he's not used to being kept waiting.

The thing about Heatherton was that he always seemed like he was on the cusp of smiling. Always on the edge of laughing, but just never got there. It was fascinating, really, to watch it all *almost happen*.

"Yeah. Yes. I mean, of course." My throat was dry and my hands were sweaty and gross. I wanted to be the one that made him laugh.

"I checked the schedule and I didn't see you working tomorrow night. Do you want to go to dinner?" He'd regained his composure. Just that fast.

"What about that scheduled ..." Appendectomy.

He cut me off. "I moved some stuff around."

He pushed a surgery - or gave it away - to date me. This was almost laughable. But I'm certainly not going to question it because - well.

*He is perfect.*

Elijah Heatherton is a 6'3" god. He is all tan - even in the dead of an Ohio winter, he's still tan. It makes me want to cuddle up to him for the warmth he exudes just by *being.*

That's a lie. I'd cuddle with him regardless of that tan.

*And so would you.*

His brown eyes are sad and his brown hair is almost always a mess because of his scrub cap. He wears Brooks running shoes almost exclusively, navy scrubs, and when he has to wear a suit? He doesn't wear a tie. He steals my pens and he blows up animal balloons for sick kids and he comforts distraught family members. And he wants a date - with *me.*

"Okay, then." I had to whisper, so scared was I that this was all a joke. Not real.

"Okay." He breathed out a huge breath. "I haven't ... done *that* in a long time. I'm a little out of practice." Another almost laugh.

"I mean - I think it was fine." I giggled at that. What even has come over the world?

"Should I pick you up at seven, then? Or ... how do you ...?" I could hear a tapping and could just see him tapping that car dealership pen on the table. I took a second to revel in the idea that Dr. Heatherton was so nervous.

"How about I meet you there." My twenties have taught me at least one thing - and that was to always drive separately to the first date. Even if it was with some kind of surgeon god.

"That sounds good." He sounded disappointed. "I was thinking about Sotto?"

Two words about Sotto, you guys. *Ricotta donuts.*

"That sounds amazing. I'll just meet you there at seven." I sounded like there was an exclamation mark at the end of every one of my words. I couldn't help it. I hung up feeling like I'd lived through some kind of excruciating/glorious five minute one hundred hard dash.

And then I turned around.

My parents were staring at me. My mom's grip on my dad's leg was so tight that her hands were white. "What ..." Her voice was rough. "Why is Dr. Heatherton calling your personal cell? Do you need to go to the hospital?" There was hope there. Hope that it was just about work.

"He wants to take me to Sotto tomorrow." I shrugged my shoulders and dove back into my place on the sectional.

"Do you think that's smart? Mixing work with your private life?" Dad's calm voice broke tension I didn't even realize was there.

"He's cute." I took a deep breath. "And, you know," I laughed. "If it all goes south, I could always just buy the hospital and fire him" That caused full on laughter - until my mom lost her own damn mind.

"Jesus, Grace. This is *serious*. You should call him back and cancel." Her eyes were hard like I'd not seen in years.

"No." I sat up to look at her more fully. "What's your deal with him?"

She huffed out. "I just think you should make better choices than Heatherton, that's all." She played with non-existent lent on her pants.

"Caroline." My dad issued a stand down order to my mother with one word. Even her posture relented. I'd been granted a reprieve.

"I got it, mom," I spoke softly.

My dad stood. "I think it's time for us to head out. Gracie? We'll see you at lunch on Sunday? Seems like we'll have a lot to talk about after you meet this ... man." He squeezed me tightly in a hug. "Remember, though," he spoke quietly. "There's a lot of changes happening in your life right now. Take slow steps."

...

I bought a new dress. I had deliveries to unpack, but I was out shopping in stores that I could actually afford. I went to Nordstrom's and the results were epic. A cute cocktail dress that did not give off the tacky, slutty nurse vibe, and new makeup.

And new shoes.

And a new clutch.

Or two.

And new undergarments because Dr. Heatherton was not a man you met in bed wearing your Thursday bra and stretched out panties.

I spent an inordinate amount of time on my unruly brown hair. The curls would just be the death of me one day. Though now, I suppose I could afford to get it chemically straightened?

Finally, it all relented and was pinned kind of neatly in place. My lacy black dress looked like a cross between a wedding with your parents and spring break drinks in Miami. How *that* is possible, only my new personal shopper, Amber, knows. I actually looked hot for once and not like an awkward teenager.

I put my strappy heels on with something akin to glee. Lawson wasn't tall enough (or brave enough) to stand by me in heels, so I stopped wearing them. It's not like he wanted me standing anyway.

When I stood in front of my mirror, I almost didn't recognize myself. I blinked a few times. My thick lashes were painted with new mascara, and my ears were glittering with new studs.

My Uber signaled he was close and I made my way down the stairs.

A date.

With a man I've been thinking about for over two years.

This could end in either one of two ways:

- He could be amazing and he could live up to everything I ever thought.
- He could climb out the bathroom window and stiff me with the check.

I would continue to pray for the first one. The second would make work incredibly awkward.

He was standing outside the restaurant when I pulled up. He was on his phone - his thumbs moving a mile a minute and I briefly wondered if it was the hospital.

The car door closed behind me just as he finished. He slid the phone into the inside of his suit jacket. Nervously, he looked around.

Nervous. Something I didn't typically associate with him.

Our eyes met across the street and he smiled at me, and do you know what?

He should *definitely* do that more often.

Carefully, I crossed the street and he greeted me with a tight hug. I swear, I could feel the warmth of his palms on my ribs.

"You are stunning. I love your dress." He looked me up and down and turned to the hostess. "I wasn't sure, you know, how you could possibly improve on those blue scrubs, but I gotta say ... you did good, Morgan." He smiled at me again and I was momentarily stunned.

He reached down and pulled on my hand. "Shall we?"

*Yes, Elijah, we shall.*

He ordered wine and he knew what he was doing.

He ordered an appetizer using impeccable Italian.

And then it was just us.

"Uh." He cleared his throat. Twice. "I, um ... I'd ask you about work, but ..."

"You already know, right?" I smiled at him. He really was struggling.

"Yeah."

I openly looked at him. He had stubble today. Like he hadn't shaved after finishing at the hospital the night before. Parts near his chin were greying. He had to be at least ten years older than me. Probably more. His watch gleamed out from under the cuff of his white button up. His teeth, perfect. His smile, when it actually appeared, was infectious.

"I'm sorry, Grace," he said, looking down at his hands. "I just ... I just never date. I don't even think I know how."

"You're doing fine so far." Impetuously, I grabbed his hand across the table. "Perhaps we should start with what brought this on?" I raised my brow at him - much like my mom had done to me a million times before ... when she was calling me out.

He smirked at me, glad to have a purpose. "A few months ago," he said softly, leaning in across the table - like he was imparting some kind of big, super secret. I couldn't help but lean closer, too. "I was elbow deep in that guy - Stevenson - elbow deep in his colon resection. I glanced up and our eyes met. You know ... I can't ... I can't ever remember being so ... *thrown* ... by just someone's eyes before ... It was like you looked at me and you just ... *saw me*." He searched for words while his thumb stroked mindlessly over mine. His hands bled warmth into me.

"And afterwards, you sat at the station and a nurse said something to you and you laughed. Just threw your head back and laughed, and I thought ... no ... I *knew* ... I wanted to be the one that made you laugh like that again."

He puffed out a breath that had been lodged in his throat for what probably seemed like months. "So ... I started paying attention. And I'm so glad I did." He looked up at me then and he was just ... devastatingly handsome.

"I'm glad you did, too." I smiled back at him and the flutters in my stomach kicked up a notch.

And then the wine came.

Conversation didn't exactly "flow". It was more of a study. Slowly, words tumbled from our lips - questions we never thought we'd get to ask, and just as he had wished, Eli - as he had asked me to call him - made me laugh over and over again.

It was fall, and when we finally left after the final ricotta donut had been eaten (by me, thankyouverymuch), some two hours later, the air was cold on my bare shoulders. He wrapped his coat around me and it smelled spicy and the sleeves were too long for my arms. Our fingers entwined and we walked with no real destination in mind.

He told me about his residency at Emory and I quietly wondered what brought him to Ohio. I talked about my parents, but easily left out all of my most important pieces of information.

"Should I take you home? I have early rounds in the morning." He looked at me and I searched those brown eyes. Regret. He didn't want to leave. I didn't either. "My car is parked down by Sotto. Do you live around here? Can I take you home?"

"I'd like that." I furrowed my brow. I had forgotten all about Ubering to the restaurant. I had to give him directions because I couldn't remember my address. We still made it, though - just as conversation actually had made it past that awkward first date phase. Naturally.

He opened the door for me and helped me out. I looked up at my building and turned to him, just as he put both of his hands on my face and pulled me in close.

"Grace Morgan," he whispered, as he dragged his stubbed filled cheek across mine. "What you do to me."

And then his lips touched mine in the most painfully perfect, soft way. Slowly, he pulled away, and I opened my eyes. If I never get kissed again - or if I get kissed a million more times - nothing will be as right as that sweet moment.

"Goodnight, Grace," he said, before kissing my cheek one last time.

"Goodnight," I whispered back. I rode the elevator up to my apartment and Lawson suddenly popped into my mind.

A side-by-side comparison appeared and Eli was the obvious winner in every way. I ruminated over Lawson as I continued to get dressed in my pajamas. What made me ever think he was worthy of me? A man so obviously using me for sex?

I slept fitfully, my dreams passing in front of my eyes - scene after scene of chaos. Lawson was Eli and Eli was ... lost.

…

Work. Day 2 Post Heatherton Date. Surgery: Aortic Aneurysm

He's elbow deep in a guy's chest and I can literally only think of how his hand felt holding mine.

He's elbow deep in a guy's chest and when he looks at me, all I can feel are prickles on my cheek from his stubble.

He's elbow deep in a guy's chest and all I really want is to be shoulder to shoulder with him again, walking down the sidewalk.

Later, I was checking on that same patient and I could swear I smelled the spiciness of his coat.

I was sitting at the nurse's station and I swore I sensed him. I rolled my eyes at myself *again*, "Stupid." I muttered. "Stupid, stupid, stupid."

A throat cleared. "Grace?"

I looked up to see the one and only Elijah and I almost threw up. "Eli," I burst out. "Er. Dr. Heatherton. Hi." I quickly looked around to see who had heard me address him so unprofessionally. No one. Thank goodness.

An almost smile. "How are you today?"

"Good?" I blinked up at him.

"Good." He started to walk away and his phone went off. After he stopped to look at it, he turned back to look at me. "I'll call you tonight?"

I could only nod. I was rendered speechless again by that ass. In those scrubs.

*Damn.*

...

Of *course* my phone rang that evening.

"Grace," he breathed out. I smiled, thankful that he hadn't blown me off like every single other frat boy that I'd ever dated.

"Hi," I sounded like I was 13 again and giggly.

"When can I see you again?" It was there - I could hear his smile.

I looked around. "Now?" If my mother were here, she'd call me reckless. "Why don't you come over? I've just gotten home. I'll shower." Okay, in my defense, our time and our schedules were cray-cray. If he was home and not at the hospital, and if I was home? I was going to capitalize and not feel bad about it - even if it did seem a little desperate.

"Have you had dinner?" I could hear some rustling in the background.

Dinner? There was popcorn in my bowl. But ... if he was going to bring me something ...

“No.” I wouldn’t say no to that.

“Perfect.” I could practically hear the gears in his head turning. “Give me an hour?”

“That sounds great. Just check in with the doorman when you get here.”

And wouldn’t you know? I was so damn focused on running for the shower that I didn’t even see the breaking news on my TV.

The Cincy Surprise Lotto Winner? Well. She was a nurse at the University Hospital.

Imagine that.

## Lesson #3

**Panic: Sudden uncontrollable fear or anxiety, often causing wildly unthinking behavior.**

**When I saw my face on the TV, I panicked like never before.**

And ... right as I was tossing my still sort of wet hair into a bun, the buzzer went off in my apartment. I dashed to the door and hit the button to allow him to come up. I decided on leggings and an old college sweater that made me feel a little more like myself. Causal, right? I'd already wowed him once. Nobody has any kind of time for twice in one week.

And spoiler: He looks just as good in jeans as he does in scrubs. I almost can't even. But I took one for the team anyway. If you were here talking to me about this, I would've just winked at you. But you're not here - thank goodness.

He walked in and took in his surroundings. "Wow. This is ... impressive." There was a question in there somewhere, but I ignored it. Maybe something like *how can you afford all of this with that view*. Or maybe *why is there still a tag hanging from the couch* ... something maybe like that?

"Thanks!" I shut the door behind him. "What did you bring?"

He had a picnic basket and it was so sweet. More importantly, though, was that it smelled delicious.

"Phillies." He put the basket on the counter and I totally intentionally brushed up against him as I walked by.

My virgin plates crashed together in the cupboard when I felt him press up behind me. "Where are the forks?" His whisper in my ear tickled. I instinctually jerked backwards. Right into him.

"In the drawer next to the sink." He pressed his lips to my neck and I was lost to him again. I was useless around him - it's amazing that I even made it to my new table.

"I didn't have time to cook tonight, so I hope these are okay." He was teasing me, I think. I liked it.

Our elbows touched and we quietly talked about our days. Maybe it was the second hearty glass of wine that I'd just polished off, or maybe it was the fact that I was all comfy and cozy in my own home, but I couldn't help it.

"Have you ever been married?" It bursted free from my mouth and sounded so loud in the stillness around us. I took a huge bite to cover it up, but part of me was thankful that I had finally asked.

He looked at me out of the corner of his eye. "I am assuming you already know the answer to that, or you wouldn't be chewing that sandwich like a terrified raccoon." He put down his fork. He finished chewing, swallowed heavily, and poured another glass of wine. I watched with bated breath.

"I was. Once. She was my college sweetheart. We married right after I matched at Emory. We went to Georgia and started to build our lives. I made it through the first year of residency and we decided it was time to have a family."

I swallowed hard and he took another huge gulp of wine.

"Sarah," he said her name like it hadn't been said in years. Like the name had to be excised from his chest. Like a nugget that is only given out on special occasions.

*Sarah.*

"Sarah was pregnant almost right away." He rubbed his hands over his eyes. "She was six months along and was going to meet me at the hospital for a quick dinner. She was late and my cell rang and it was her. She had a flat tire on the side of the highway and it was raining, so I left the hospital to go help her." The words fell out of his mouth robotically. Like he'd told the story a million times.

He stared at the wall and I stared at his mouth ... willing him to continue. Begging him to continue in my head. Desperately needing to hear the rest of the story.

"I got to her car and ... Sarah. She was so headstrong. She was standing on the side of the road trying to get the lug nuts off by herself. Her hair was stuck to her forehead. I ... I'll never forget that." He leaned forward and put his elbows on the table and I wanted to scream at him and ask where his baby was.

"I chided her. Told her to get back in the car. And damn if she'd listen to me. The rain just kept coming. We had to yell to hear over it and the traffic. And I needed a flashlight. I told her to move - to stand away from the road. So ..." He cleared his throat. "She moved ... She moved in between our two cars. I turned around on the way back to my car and she smiled back at me. Typical of her, you know?" No. I didn't know, but he wasn't here with me. He was back there and the far away look in his eye told me not to intrude on this particular moment. "She was wet. Cold. Pregnant. Out in the rain. And she wasn't even mad." He cleared his throat again - back with me now, I suppose.

"It happened ... *so fast*." He shifted in his seat. "The kid driving the other car was in college. Drunk. He slammed into the back of my car, which slammed into ..." He trailed off.

*Sarah.*

"It slammed into Sarah. The force of the impact threw me into the ditch. When I came to, there were people ... everywhere. Paramedics. Ambulances. Fire trucks. Police. Everywhere. The kid was dead. And Sarah. Sarah was laying on the trunk of her car, pinned. I shoved through the crowd. Jesus. I am a doctor, you know? Trained to save lives. My wife's life. My baby's life. *Trained*." His words were coming out hard and hateful. I reached across the table and held on to his cold hand.

"She didn't die until we got to the hospital. They all tried so hard to save her. But neither of them ... Neither of them could hang on." He swallowed again, and reached for the stem of his wine glass.

"I took time off to ... to bury them. I finished my residency. And then, I came here. Away. Far away from the people at Emory that knew all of my story. Far away from the questions - the pity. Far away from the doctors that tried to save them, but couldn't. Far away from the guilt that I saw in their eyes every single time I saw them. I came here. Far away from her ... her memory. She was just ... *everywhere* there. She had touched all of the parts of my life, and so I had to go. Had to get away."

He nodded once and looked at me. "So yes. Married. Once."

And I thought about all of the almost smiles and the almost laughs and realized that he was still trying to walk his way home.

"Okay." It was all I could say that didn't sound trite or used up or saccharine.

"Okay." He repeated. And then, more for himself, "Okay."

We continued eating in silence, waiting for an equilibrium to settle back over us.

I felt red in my ledger. I felt like the scale was uneven. It felt like he had just imparted huge wisdom - a huge piece of him that no one else knew about. And those worry lines around those sad brown eyes and those hands and the way it felt in my tummy when he kissed me.

Well.

It all felt like trust.

"I won the Cincinnati lottery." I said it so quietly that I wondered if he had even heard me.

He *did* laugh at that. "You don't have to try to cheer me up. I'm good. Really." He patted my leg and smiled at me. He laughed again. I did not.

"I'm serious, Elijah." Maybe it was the way I'd said his name, or maybe it was the way I pulled my hand away from his.

It was a bad idea. You don't have to tell me that. I've lived through enough bad ideas in my life to recognize one when I see it. As soon as I'd uttered the words, I realized how tragically bad of an idea it was to tell a man on date two that I'm a billionaire anonymous lottery winner.

My dad would be appalled.

And so would Sean.

Whatever.

Eli looked up at me. "You're not kidding, are you?"

"Nope." I gestured around. "Who do you know that can afford brand new everything at 25?"

He looked around as if he was seeing everything again for the first time. "Holy shit, Grace."

Yeah. That's what I said, too.

"So now you know why I've been distracted." I shrugged my shoulders.

He looked over at me and smiled. "This whole time I thought it was a guy." He reached for my hand again. "This place is nice." He appraised my new couch.

"Wanna watch a movie on that couch?" I raised my eyebrow at him.

"I was sort of hoping to skip that and move straight into making out." He winked at me and I think I would've agreed to anything.

And so we did. We moved to the couch after I turned down the lights and it was perfect. His lips were soft and his hands massaged my scalp as his tongue explored my mouth, my ear lobes, and my neck. My hands smoothed over his chest and shoulders, and felt the friction of his stubble along my palms.

His hands dropped to my thighs and the ensuing squeeze left me almost paralyzed with some kind of wild need. He could've asked me to do anything in that moment. Could've asked me to my bedroom and could've asked me to drop my pants. I would've gladly submitted.

But slowly, his kisses eased in intensity. "We should slow down. Unless ... you're ready, but we should slow down." He kissed that magic spot behind my ear again. "At least wait until date three." He softly chuckled. "Grace," he whispered slowly. "When can I see you again?" Another kiss to my neck. Under my chin. On top of my lips.

"Soon." My voice sounded foreign even to me. Rough.

He pushed some hair back from my eyes, and kissed my forehead. "Good." He pulled back again. "I should go before this gets ... much more out of control."

We both stood and righted our somehow askew clothes. By the door, I held on for dear life as he kissed me hard again. "I'll check my schedule at work tomorrow. Will I see you at the hospital?"

I smiled up at him. "Of course." I had every intention of being at work the next day - and the week after. But while I was making out with the good doctor, my phone was imploding.

The news had officially broke.

I was no longer anonymous in my city.

The press was camped out under my apartment window and Sean and my parents had to shove their way through the next morning to get to me.

"What the hell happened?" Sean bellowed at me when I opened the door. "Who can't keep their mouth shut?" He stared accusingly at us.

## Lesson #4

**Trust: Firm belief in the reliability, truth, ability, or strength of *someone* or something**

**My mom trusted her best friend, but not anymore.**

"I didn't say a word, Sean," I was vehement. No way could Eli rain this down and I told no one else. Not even my closest friends.

My mom quietly started a pot of coffee and I stood by the window. "And now I'm trapped. Everyone will know. Know me." My phone didn't stop ringing and dinging all night long. I eventually just shut it off and threw it in the guest bedroom.

"Then how in the hell did this happen?" He looked around at the three of us. "Randolph? Caroline? Did either of *you* say anything?" The air thickened and slowly, I turned my head to my parents. No way.

My dad cleared his throat. "Caroline?" My head snapped to my mom.

"Are you kidding me? I'm a prisoner in my own home because of my own *mother*?" I crossed my arms, my eyes widened.

My mom nodded at me. "I told Sabrina."

Fucking *Sabrina.*

My mom's oldest friend. Like Sean, she'd been around my family since the Dark Ages.

"Damn it." I would've been pissed had it been anyone else. But Sabrina. Well. She's practically my second mother.

"Why? Why would she?" I couldn't imagine someone betraying me - or my own mother - like that.

"SHE didn't. Her husband did. She told him that night. She was so happy for you. From there, I think Tab told a partner at his firm. And the rest ... is history."

Now Tab? Totally different story. Where Sabrina is everything good and true, Tab is just ... a dick. And he uses his on every single thing that moves. Yet Sabrina stays. She's old school steel. She'll never leave.

"Fucking Tab." I turned back to the window. High off the ground. Away from everyone and everything and I was a literally prisoner in a fortress that I paid rent for.

Sean sighed at the same time my beleaguered door man buzzed.

"Miss Morgan," a voice called out. "A Dr. Heatherton?"

I don't know how much doormen make, but mine sure deserved a raise.

"Yes," I answered him. "Send him up." I looked at my astonished family. "He knows," was all I supplied.

"What if it was him?" My dad clipped out, and then huffed furiously.

"He found out *after* the news broke." I looked pointedly at my mom. "Be nice."

She was affronted, I could tell. "I'm always nice."

"I like this man. A lot. Be freaking nice." The doorbell saved me from her reply. I had never been quite so ... demanding before. She was probably not going to let me off the hook for it, either.

Sean opened the door to a bewildered Elijah, who carried two coffees. Thank the ever living Lord. "Hi," he said to the room. I took a coffee and a quick, restorative hug. He held out his hand to my dad. "Elijah Heatherton."

Dad eyed him in that spectacular way that only dads can, and then held out his own hand. "Morgan."

Sean stepped forward. "Sean Graves. Grace's attorney. Are you the boyfriend?"

I think my eyes popped out of my head. Here I was worried about my mother, but nope - it was Sean. Sean was the one that was actually going to kill me today.

I said no at the same time Eli said yes. I gaped at him.

"Caroline Morgan." My mother stepped forward. "I work on the peds floor at Cincy University."

Eli shook her hand. "I thought I recognized you. Good to meet you." He rocked back on his heels as an awkward silence descended.

"So ... everyone knows? Grace? I swear I didn't say a word to anyone. You have to believe that." His eyes implored me.

"I do," but I was still wondering how I became Dr. Heatherton's girlfriend.

Sean stepped forward. "Just in case ... we'd like you to sign a non-disclosure. I don't know how close you are with Grace," he gave me one hell of a side eye, "but this should be signed before things go too much further." Sean went to his briefcase.

"Of course." Eli took another sip of coffee. "Whatever you need me to do."

He and Sean stood at the counter, reviewing the particulars and I stared at the two of them. My *boyfriends* were now required to sign non-disclosure agreements. My attorney was outlining things he could and couldn't talk about in my kitchen.

This. This is my life now.

My mom stood next to me. "I'm sorry, Gracie." She put her arm around my waist.

"It's okay," I muttered. "I think I knew the secret couldn't stay hidden forever."

"He really *is* handsome," she whispered.

"And a gentleman. And kind." I looked at her. "And he likes me."

"Oh, Gracie," she smiled softly. "What's not to like?"

"Are you going to quit your job?" My dad now stared out the window, but I knew he was talking to me.

"No. Why would I? What else would I do every day?" *Anything* but become a real prisoner here, I prayed quietly.

"You can't go through that every day - what's downstairs." He motioned ten floors down.

"Surely they'll move on." Right? "Surely I can't be news forever."

"I think you'll need to give them something." Sean looked up as Eli signed the document in front of him. "An interview. A statement. Something."

"What *is* the plan?" Eli capped his pen and took a swig of coffee. It was not lost on me that he had just signed an NDA to be with me and hadn't even batted an eye.

"I don't think we have one yet." I looked around. "Anyone have any awesome ideas?"

Around me, everyone was silent.

Sean cleared his throat and everyone looked his way. "I know a woman in Public Relations. She's good. I've never had to use her, but a couple of guys at the firm swear by her. I could call her in for an emergency meeting?" He raised his eyebrows.

"That would've been a great idea ... like *yesterday*, Sean," my mother playfully scolded him.

"Sorry, Caro ... this is the only time I've ever really had to represent a 25-year-old billionaire lottery winner. I'm a little rusty here." He turned and pulled out his cell. "Give me a sec."

Eli stared at me wide-eyed.

"Welcome to the show," I said half-heartedly.

"Can't wait to see how it plays out." And there it was. His full on smile. My mother gasped next to me.

Yeah, mom. SEE?

It took less than an hour for Megan Rhodes to show up. She burst through the doors with gusto and didn't stop for a second. Much younger than I would've guessed, Megan was dressed impeccably and was well-prepared. "Grace Morgan?" She held her hand out to me. "Megan Rhodes. Pleasure to meet you."

Sean stepped up next to her. "Megan. I'm Sean. We spoke on the phone. We're having everyone from outside Grace's inner circle sign an NDA. If you're unwilling to do that now, we won't be proceeding." She quickly read over the document and signed. Then, she turned her unnerving gaze to me.

"How can I help?"

Sean spoke again. "What -"

Megan didn't take her eyes off of me. "Grace. How can I help you?" Only then did she look at Sean to acknowledge him. "She's going to need to learn to speak and to speak well. She possesses more money now than three fourths of the world, Mr. Graves. The Cincy press isn't the only thing she has to worry about."

"Tell me what to do." I stared at this *force* of a woman.

"No. You're missing the point. You call the shots. You want an interview? I'll set one up. You don't? I'll send a press release and organize a press barrier." She paused and looked me over. "You need to figure out a path."

What kind of convoluted bullshit was this? "Isn't your *job* to tell me what to do here?"

"No." Her voice rang out clear in my apartment. "I suspect you've been told your whole life. My *job* is to *advise* you. Tell me what *you* want to do and I'll counsel you from there."

My parents sat in stunned silence.

"What will make them all go away out front?" I gestured feebly towards the windows. In her presence, I somehow felt like *less*. Like my shit was definitely not together ... but she made me *want* to feel get it together. She was good and I wasn't even sure I knew how or why yet.

"An interview." She crossed her arms, waiting for my decision.

"I don't know how to be 'interviewed'." I blinked at her.

"I'll teach you." She glanced at her watch.

"Okay." I shrugged my shoulders. I guess I could learn that. She could give me lessons, or ... something.

"Rule one, Grace Morgan. Be explicit in your instructions. *Okay* and complacency are no longer a thing. You always hold the key. *You* always get to decide. It's time to rise. So what does 'okay' actually mean?" She was some kind of pit bull in $600 shoes.

I cleared my throat. Sean hired a ballbuster. "I'd like to give an interview."

She sighed. "We'll have to work on that, I guess." She motioned at me. Turning, she walked away and to the dining room to set up some sort of make-shift command center.

"Work on what?" I asked. Everyone around me seemed just as clueless.

"Your presence, Grace. You need to take up space. Own your voice. You wouldn't 'like' an interview. You 'want' an interview. Right now." She opened her computer bag and pulled out files. Shuffling through them, she found a piece of paper, and dialed a number. "Yes. Hi. Megan Rhodes. I'm representing Grace Morgan." She sighed. "Yes. I'll hold."

Eli walked over to me while she was on the phone. "Grace." His voice was soft in my ear. "I have a patient at two and another at six. I need to get to the hospital. Do you want me to push them?"

"No." *That* I didn't even have to think about. "Go. I understand."

He kissed my forehead. "Can I come back tonight?"

"Yes. Please do." I breathed out some anxiety. "Maybe we'll have made some headway by then." I smiled weakly at him. "And maybe we can sit on my couch again."

He kissed me again. "I'd like that a lot." He said goodbye to my parents and Sean, and then let himself out.

"Grace Morgan," Sean chided. "Who is that man?" Sean. Good ol' Sean. The man that's had to rescue me from a high tower once or twice. He sounded hurt.

"Dr. Heatherton," my mother supplied. "Head of General Surgery at Cincy University."

"Let her answer for herself," Megan called from the table. "She needs the practice."

"He's my boyfriend." I tried the word on. "And he's ... perfect." *That* was a good word fit.

"What's that mean?" Megan dialed another number and hardly looked up from her work. "Be more specific, Grace, or don't say anything at all."

I rolled my eyes at her, even though she couldn't see it. "He brought me coffee and he's a good kisser and he opens my car door. There. Are you happy?" I glared at her.

"I'd be happier if you had left out the kissing part. Hello, this is Megan Rhodes." Her attention was diverted and I breathed a sigh of relief.

"Well." Sean put his hands into his pockets. "I'm glad ... you're happy."

"Very." I nodded my head once.

"No. Just say thank you." Megan called again.

"Thank you," I amended. She was already exhausting.

My dad had the nerve to laugh.

"Shut up, Randolph." I flipped him off.

"I'm glad it's my daughter with the money and not me. I couldn't handle the handler." Still chuckling, he gestured over to the pitbull at the table.

"You'll think that come nursing home time. Just remember who pulls the strings." I huffed on the couch.

"Gracefully ... *Grace*." Megan raised her hands to Jesus.

"You can shut up, too." I stared her down.

Megan punched a fist into the air and hung up her phone. "YES! There's our girl!" She stood and walked over to me.

"People are going to push at you. That place right there where you just told me to shut up? That's the place you walk with. Head up. Shoulders back. Cut the mousey crap." She waved her pen at me.

"I don't even know what mousey means." I nearly erupted. "Stop calling me that."

Megan only smiled. "Good."

I flopped back down on the couch. "I'm starving."

"No time to eat, kid. Go and get dressed. You have a sit down at two." She nearly shoved me into my bedroom. "Nicer clothes than those, please. And do something with that hair."

I touched my hair. "The fuck is wrong with my hair?"

"Yeah, and not the word fuck in public either. Get dressed. I'll prep your family." She left me in the blessed quiet of my room.

I took a deep, deep breath. I could do this. I knew I could do this. It took a hot second, but I came out of my room looking like a goddess compared to how I normally look. I interrupted the pow wow happening in the kitchen.

"And those records are sealed?" Megan was asking.

Sean was stoic. "Yes. She was a minor. We kept it as quiet as possible."

I stood in the hallway as my past once again came roaring back to life.

"We don't even discuss it anymore." My mother was whispering. She was my protector. She was adamant. "We've moved on."

"Good." Megan looked up. "Grace. You look ... better. Are you ready?"

I could only nod.

"We're meeting the press in the conference room downstairs. I'm going to need you to verbalize you're good to go." She eyed me speculatively.

I took a deep breath and retreated back to the solace of my new bathroom.

This wasn't me.

My ears were roaring.

I didn't have a public relations expert in my dining room.

What kind of life was I living? Or *whose* life was I living?

My breath sped up and I recognized the panic attack as it came on full force. I greeted it as the old friend it was. I pushed the lid down on my toilet and sat down heavily. I shoved my head between my legs. Visions from the last few months leapt across my eyelids - like someone else was living the same life as me. I felt so detached. My breathing was heavy and loud and the space was small and hot.

But I forced myself to breathe.

To take deep, gasping, full breaths.

Count to ten and then back to one.

To ten and back to one.

To ten.

I felt a hand on my back and expecting my mother - the woman who had witnessed countless other attacks - I raised my head. My eyes closed, I whispered that I just *couldn't.*

"Yes, you can," Megan's soft voice echoed off of the close walls. She rubbed my back when I bent back over. I must've looked a mess. "Breathe, Grace. It's okay." She continued to rub my back and neither of us spoke.

"I'm not a press conference kind of girl," I said, wiping tears from my eyes.

"Which is why I'm here. I'll help you." Small circles on my back. Her hand was soothing and rhythmic. "You sit in that chair and you hold the power, Grace. You answer what you want, or you don't comment. You're done? Get up and leave and I'll deal with them from there. You are not wilting flower. Don't act like one." The rubbing stopped and she patted my shoulder. "Take five more minutes."

Not a wilting flower. Not a wilting flower.

I took deep breaths.

And instead of just taking five more minutes, I took fifteen.

We headed out the door to the elevator and my dad grasped my hand. "You can do this, Gracie-girl."

*Yeah,*I thought, *I'd believe that when I see it.*

In the quiet lobby, Megan stopped us. "I'll go in first, prep them, and then come back out for you. Now listen," she said quietly. "They're going to ask you about spending and charity. If you don't know, say you don't, and I'll call the next reporter out. Remember, you're in control here. Not them." She nodded once and her heels clacked across the tiled floor.

"Jesus, Sean. You brought in a brute." My mother heaved out a sigh. "We can find someone else if you want, Grace."

"No." I surprised even myself. "She stays."

And just like that, I felt myself rise.

"Just for the record and all - I hired the *best*." Sean's voice was full in the empty area. I smiled.

In the end, Megan was right - as she would be time and time again in the coming year. All they really cared about was what I bought first (Starbucks), what kind of good I was going to do (undecided), and if I was going to quit my job (no). I felt like I handled their questions with aplomb, and when Megan said last question, the relief washed over me.

"Are you dating anyone?" A question was called out from the back.

Just as I answered yes, Megan spoke up, "My client doesn't comment on her dating life." The room laughed, I shrugged my shoulders, and Megan smiled tightly. Who knew? Certainly not me.

The elevator ride back up to my apartment was quiet. When we were finally inside, I kicked off my heels and Megan started. "Never, and I do mean *never* comment again on your dating life. Then, that person becomes a target, too. Just keep quiet about that stuff. Otherwise, remarkable job."

I rolled my eyes. "You should've *led* with good job." I went to the door. "I'm done for the day, Megan. It's been a ... *treat*." I opened the door, signaling her time was up for the day.

"Yes." The bitch smiled like I was doing exactly what she expected me to. "I think so, too." She turned to Sean. "It was my pleasure, Sean." She actually kissed his cheek and my dad covered his laugh remarkably well with a couch. "Call me when you need me again." And then she was gone and I exhaled.

"Come on, Sean. Surely there is someone else?" My dad sounded so tired. Like he was carrying this, too. And *this* was freaking heavy.

I slumped into the couch - which was quickly becoming my refuge. "Okay. She stays. She's the only one that seems to be able to bear this at all.

Sean?" He raised his eyes to me, a blush was still faintly coloring his cheeks. "Do we like her? Do I pay her? How does that work?"

"Well," he mused. "I could draw up a contract. Go from there. Have Marshall add her to your payroll?"

I had a payroll? "Who is on my *payroll*?" I was incredulous. How I had I not thought to ask?

"Grace. Surely you don't think Sean is working for free?" My mother's voice was cautious.

## Lesson #5

**Ignorance: Lack of knowledge or information**

**Bliss: Perfect happiness; great joy**

Ignorance is *not* bliss.

When I was 16, my best friend, Sadie, had a baby. I didn't even know she was pregnant. And I was her *best friend.* Our parents were best friends. We'd literally grown up together. We were all family.

Maybe she didn't know she was pregnant, either.

Maybe she was in denial, too.

Maybe we all were.

But it happened.

She delivered the baby in her bathroom. The pink and white bathroom that had Anne Gedes baby pictures hanging from the wall. She delivered a baby and she wrapped it carefully in a bed sheet and she took it outside and she buried in the creek bed behind her house.

She buried her baby.

And she told no one for two weeks.

We were laying on her bed one afternoon and we were talking about how she had just broken up with her boyfriend. That's when she told me.

So casually.

Like she was reporting the weather.

Or math facts from algebra class.

Like she was asking what color my prom dress was, or who she should chase after next.

She killed her baby and she was blasé.

Something shifted then. In me. In my life.

I asked her about the details and she rattled them right off.

"It didn't even hurt that bad." She laughed.

I wanted to ask which part didn't hurt.

The baby?

The killing?

The placing a living thing in a box and putting it in the same creek sand that we had played in when we were four-years-old?

I sat through dinner. Her mother - the woman I'm named after - talked about the church bazaar she was planning, about her ladies night out group, and she fused over how much I wasn't eating. Lawrence, Sadie's dad, talked about stocks and the garden they were going to plant, and how he couldn't wait for grilling season. Sadie talked about freaking bible study and her math teacher. I pushed peas around my plate and vomit back down my throat. I helped with the dishes, and when I said I needed to go home?

Sadie was worried about me. Said I looked sick. Said she hoped I didn't have that stomach bug that was going around. Felt my forehead with her cold hands and I trembled as she touched me.

I don't even remember driving home. I don't even remember finding my dad in his study. I don't even remember telling him.

I remember rocking back and forth on the couch. My dad helping me to the car. On the drive back to Sadie's, my mother sobbed in the front seat. My stoic father - he had pulled a shovel off of the wall in the garage. When we pulled into the driveway, my mom turned to me one more time. "You're sure she wasn't lying?" But who would lie about something so devastating?

We were on the edge of something. I could feel it. If Sadie was lying, the relationship our parents had would never recover. We were talking about decades of friendship. Down the drain after this; there was no turning back.

I can remember how cold the car felt after my dad turned it off. "Mom. I hope she was. Right? I hope she was lying."

The three of us got out of the car and my dad grabbed his shovel. Lawrence met us at the door. "Morgan? What ..." He trailed off at the sight of dad's shovel and our visibly upset demeanor. "What happened?"

Just then, I heard this shift in his voice. He experienced the life shift, too. Nothing would ever be the same for Lawrence and Grace Traverty. Never again.

"I need to check your creek. You should come." My dad didn't wait for an answer.

"You should find your wife." My mother's voice was as hard as I'd ever heard and the fact that she didn't use her oldest friend's name, said something to the bewildered Lawrence.

"She's baking banana bread in the kitchen." He started after my dad. "And Sadie is upstairs working on her homework."

The house should've smelled good, but forever, the smell of banana bread would be burned into my head. For the rest of my life, it will roll my stomach. Grace was humming *The Old Rugged Cross*, but stopped when she turned and saw us.

"My God. What's happened?" She had on polka dotted oven mitts.

"Was Sadie pregnant, Grace?" I snapped my head to my mother. I thought she'd ease her in. Start slow, but just beyond her, I could see my dad digging with a shovel. I knew she'd seen him, as well.

Sadie had done that, too.

Must've pushed a shovel into the damp earth.

A box on the ground with a baby inside.

Did she sweat? Was she winded?

Did she dig deep enough?

Tears sprung into Grace's eyes. "What? No. Of course not." She pulled her oven mitts off. "What's going on here?"

"Sadie told Grace that she delivered a baby in her bathroom two weeks ago. I'll ask again. Was she pregnant?" My mom took a step closer to the other woman.

In front of me, she turned white. “Her ... her bathroom? What? A baby?”

I heard footsteps hammer down the stairs and there was Sadie.

“Hi, Mrs. Morgan. Gracie? Are you okay? Mom?” She stopped dead in her tracks and just behind her, I could see Lawrence and my dad holding a shoe box.

Opening a shoe box.

Closing a shoe box.

My dad threw up into the creek.

“Oh my God.” Sadie’s voice brought me back to the kitchen. “YOU FUCKING TOLD THEM?” She screamed and the sound reverberated around the kitchen.

“Sadie. You will not use that language inside this house.” Grace was furious.

*A little late to be pissed about language,* I thought.

“I did,” I choked out, finally. “I told them.”

The deck doors opened and a stricken Lawrence was holding the box.

“Grace. You need to come here.” He eyed his daughter with a strange look of contempt mixed with fear.

Oh, the Travertys loved their daughter. That’s for sure. But they also loved Jesus. And if they had nothing else, they still had the knowledge of what was right and what was wrong. And this was wrong.

Grace caressed the shoe box. “Is that ...”

“Yes. We need to call Sean. And the police.” He faltered. “We need to tell them that ... our ... our baby killed ...” He coughed. “Killed her baby.”

The rest was a haze.

Sadie flew into some kind of wild rage and my poor father - stunned and heartbroken for his goddaughter - had to restrain her.

Sean came first.

His wheels squealed in the driveway.

Sadie was still screaming about betrayal in the kitchen.

The police came next.

They took her away in handcuffs, and the Travertys followed her to the police station.

She had done harm. Wrong. But she was their daughter. And so they went.

The baby was taken away to the morgue where an autopsy would be carried out.

"Faith," as she'd been named later, died of asphyxiation. She was buried eventually in the Traverty family plot.

The hearing was blessedly quick. My testimony was sealed because I was a minor. No one would ever have to know that I even had been a witness.

But it would stay. Stay on my shoulders. It would stay with me forever.

Sadie was placed in a juvenile detention center for two years - until she turned 18. She was still currently serving the rest of her thirty year sentence at the state penitentiary.

I continued to live my life. I graduated. I went to the same nursing school as my mother.

And my parents? Well, "protective over their child" snowballed into some kind of weird all-encompassing bubble life.

Friends were lost in the fray. I lived with my mom and dad and kept my head down. I regressed to being a twelve-year-old again. If I couldn't even trust my best friend, who could I trust? Certainly not my judgment.

Caroline and Randolph were my saviors and throughout that radical time in my life, and they became my biggest enablers. They stepped lightly around me, terrified that at any moment I would crack. Eventually, we started to regain our footing. I finished college and found a job and a crappy apartment and we were living life. Normal life. The three of us. I would call on them for *normal* help. They would provide parental counseling and support. We were making it through.

And then the lottery happened and the idea of *support* became confusing, I suppose. For so long, my parents have been a shield and a barrier and a protective arm around my shoulders. And now, well.

I have a payroll that I don't know about.

"Who is on my payroll?" I asked again. I have lived some long days in my life. This was turning out to be one of them.

Dad sighed. "Sean. Marshall Graves. Now Megan." He looked at me. "And probably your doorman after all of this today."

Okay. Three people. I wasn't quite at Kardashian status yet. Three people I could handle. Three people seemed normal. A lawyer, a money guy, and a PR person. Normal.

Or.

New normal?

Maybe it's just manageable.

Sean's phone rang and he walked back to the dining room.

"Did you tell Megan about Sadie?" My eyes stared at the wall of windows in front of me. "Does she know?"

My mom stood and came to the windows beside me. "Yes. But I don't think it really matters, Gracie. It's done and over with. I think the only thing people care about here is that you won money - not what ghosts you've got in your closet."

"And any sane person will understand that they aren't *your* ghosts, Grace." My dad's low, calm voice washed over me. He was trying to drive home the point that he always did - the same thing that I still grappled with. She was my best friend. I should've known.

I took a deep breath. "I -"

...was cut off by Sean.

"That was Megan. The stories are all running on the four, five, and six o'clock news, with a re-run on the ten o'clock. She expects newspaper articles to continue through the week and into next, possibly, but she thinks that'll be the end."

The relief in the room was palpable. "What about the people outside?" I looked down below at the news vans.

"On her way out, she noticed that many of them were beginning to pack up." Sean shrugged his shoulders. "Want me to go down and check?"

"I'll go with you," my dad spoke up and started to get off of the couch.

"I think I'm going to go take a nap." Suddenly, my bones were even tired and my eyelids were heavy.

"Maybe that's a good idea, Grace. You've had a big day. Why don't I make some dinner?" She glanced at the kitchen and then at the fridge. Surely she realized that I wouldn't have a stocked fridge. "Or maybe I'll order something."

I only nodded and headed to my new bed with my new sheets. I yanked back the duvet and sunk down into the comfort of a pillow top mattress and flannel pillow cases. The days would get easier, I repeated over and over to myself. I either eventually believed myself, or sleep finally found me. I dreamed about shoeboxes.

...

His hand dragged up my thigh and then I smelled that same spicy smell from his shirt. And then, he was there, laying behind me, and pressing his body in closer to mine. I could tell through the haze in my bedroom that it was evening and my blankets were soft and warm and ... *he was with me*. I rolled over.

"Hi," I whispered, my eyes still not even open. The nap was just the restorative kind that a girl needs after a long day. My tummy grumbled and I could smell something delicious coming from the kitchen.

"Hi," he whispered back, his voice soft and gravelly. "Your mom ordered takeout. Are you hungry?"

"Mmmhm," I murmured. Instead of getting up, I buried my nose into his soft t-shirt. "You always smell good."

I felt his lips drop to my head. "So do you." He nuzzled his face in my hair and his hand rubbed up and down my back.

"How was the hospital?" I snuggled in closer, dinner and my parents forgotten.

"Everyone had a question today." He sighed. I totally understood.

"Samesies."

His hand dipped under the waistband of my yoga pants and if was even possible, I pulled him in tighter to me. The air around us became charged and my breath quickened. His palm drifted across my lower back until his thumb rubbed over my hip bone. The light touch flipped some kind of switch on my internal circuit board and my nails dug into his back.

Sigh.

And then there was a crash in the kitchen and I could feel the moment slip away.

"We should go join your parents for dinner. I think they're going to head home after. So ..." The end of his sentence held a wealth of possibility.

I could only nod, not even one bit ashamed of the fact that I was about to drop my drawers fifteen feet away from where my dad was probably watching ESPN on the couch.

Eli stood and pulled me up, too. He righted my somehow askew pants and tucked hair back behind my ear. "You know you snore?"

My eyes widened in embarrassment. "Shut the hell up. I do not."

He shrugged his shoulders and almost smiled. "You do." He pushed me forward towards the living room and smacked my ass for good measure. "I'm starving."

We walked out of my bedroom and my cheeks flushed. For some reason I felt like we'd been caught, but my mother just looked up from the counter and smiled. And she looked at Eli like she adored him. Talk about an about face. I just blinked at her and she shrugged.

"Italian?" She raised her eyebrows and scooped some kind of cheesy/noodle-y goodness onto a plate for me and my dad uncorked a bottle of wine. Together, the four of us sat around my table and decompressed.

The night sky of Cincinnati came down around us and the lights of the city twinkled out my living room windows. We finished off two bottles of wine and all of the Tiramisu. Eli talked about the hospital a little and we all decided it was best if maybe I just used my remaining vacation and stayed home for a week or two. It would give me more time to get my will in order (whatever that would entail), and maybe the press would die down a little.

Eventually, after my momma's twelfth yawn, dad helped her into her jacket and the went home. She stood in the doorway, hugged me goodbye, and shocked the holy hell out of me when she hugged Eli, too.

"I'll call you tomorrow," I told her as the door was closing. I had no idea what caused her to shift her stance on Eli, but I wasn't sad about it.

When the door shut behind my parents, I turned to look at the man standing next to me. He had on dark jeans and funky dress socks. His shirt was olive green and it did all the good things for his eyes. His hair was messy - eternally so - and his eyes were staring right back at me.

"Should we clean up the mess in the kitchen?" His feet didn't budge from the cool tile.

"No," I whispered. My heart in my throat. My stomach in knots. My hands sweating. My mouth dry. I shook my head slightly.

His hand reached for mine as he took a tentative step forward. "Grace," his voice came out like a prayer. Low. Intimate.

"Yes?" My eyes closed as his arms wrapped around my waist. I rested my head on his chest and his heart thundered in my ear. My hands slid around to his back and you know what?

Leaning into him kinda felt like leaning into home.

"I haven't ..." He cleared his throat, and I knew what he was going to say. "I haven't since ..."

"Sarah?"

He cleared his throat again. "Yes."

No pressure or anything, right? Because the last guy I'd slept with was some lame ass, beef jerky eating, Sharknado expert that marched in the women's march solely to pick up "the easy ones". I go from that? To Eli. God of the scalpel and wounded widower. A could-be scrubs model and a dad that had to bury his wife and child. I had no bearings. No foothold. No perspective. No mature way to handle any of this, so -

"We should just do it really fast the first time. You know. Get it out of the way?"

Word vomit.

THAT I would always be spectacular at.

He chuckled into my hair. "Or we could go slow?" His hand traveled up my back and goosebumps broke out over my arms. He pushed his fingers through my hair and held my face and kissed me.

Slowly.

His lips tasted like red wine and somedays and I liked his slow idea much better than my fast idea.

Before I even really knew what happened, we were halfway across my apartment - headed straight for my bedroom. His footsteps sure and slow, one arm tightly around my hips and the other hand stroking my chin and neck and hair. He calmed my crazy, my wild, and my shaking hands. He was sure. He was easy. But ...

Slow? Slow was driving me crazy.

The light from the bathroom cast my bedroom in shadows and for a second, we both stood by my bed staring at each other.

Willing the other to move.

Standing on some kind of wild precipice.

## Lesson #6

**Sex: Sexual intercourse**

**A herd of wild boars couldn't stop me from having sex with that man.**

And, so ... we jumped.

He dropped his hands to the hem of my shirt and with an easy tug, off it came over my head. My hands drifted down the front of his hard chest, and his shirt, too, came off. My jaw dropped at the sight of his tan torso.

He pulled my body close to his and the warmth that radiated from his body would be enough to keep me warm for the next sixty years. And like some kind of expert that you only see on YouTube, my bra was on the ground. He trailed his thumb across my collar bone and then down my shoulder. His eyes never left mine and the rise and fall of his chest quickened as his hand skirted around the bottom of my breast.

"You're beautiful," he whispered, and something deep inside recognized that raw honesty. The words were out of his mouth before he even thought to stop them.

I tugged on his brown leather belt and unbuttoned his jeans. All in, right? Slowly, my hands dipped under the elastic waistband of his boxers and his jeans slid with an easy thud to the ground. My eyes didn't stray from his this time, and smiling, he pushed my pants down, too.

Again, he kissed me in a languid sort of way that made me think that was all we were going to do for the rest of our lives. He explored every part of my mouth. He sucked on my lips and tongue. Bit my earlobe, and dragged his salt and pepper stubble across my neck.

By the time the back of my legs hit the bed, I didn't know whether to shout for joy or cry because making out with him would be over for a second. I crawled in and flashed my most provocative come hither look at him over my shoulder and damn if I didn't have a little bit of a heart attack.

The light shining from the bathroom had illuminated his face and casted a shadow around his body. He stood as still as a statue and for a second, I wasn't sure if any of this was real.

"Grace," he whispered again. And just like that, I was on my back. He pushed my wrists into the soft mattress and grinded his hips into me.

There are moments that define a girl's life, you know? There are moments that girls carry with them forever. Moments that they pull out and measure others against. Moments that become their barometer. They hold them up to the light and they say, "This one. This is the one that was the best. This is the one that you will have to beat."

For me? When I felt the full weight of that man's body on my own, I knew perfection. I knew that I would spend the rest of my life trying to find Another One to measure up to Eli. When my name fell from his lips in some kind of ragged whisper of a prayer, a place on my heart was completely and irrevocably tattooed with his hot breath, his soft lips, and his quiet confidence.

And as corny as it sounds - as cliched, and as stupid-story-book-ish - when he slipped into me and when his hips pushed into me over and over again, I knew what home felt like. Home was not the house that my mom and dad had built, or the bedroom with the soft purple walls and old bedspread. Home was not Sunday afternoon dinners. No. Home, now, was this man. His sculpted shoulders that flexed with every thrust, and his warm hands that tightened around mine, and the unwavering irises that never left mine.

My world shifted.

And everything blissfully fell away for a second.
It was four a.m. when his phone pager when off. I cuddled into his back as he called the hospital. He was warm and I was warm and my new bed and pretty new sheets were comfortable.

"Dr. Heatherton," his husky voice called out into the dawning light. He grunted a few mhmms. Asked about vitals. And breathed a heavy sigh.

I pulled back enough to give him some space because that was a sigh I'd heard before in the operating room. Something was not quite right. He was headed back to the hospital.

He ended his call and rolled into me. His lips found my neck and that sweet spot behind my ear. "I have to go," he whispered. It was almost like he didn't want to break whatever magic spell we'd both created together the night before. It was almost as if speaking any louder would mean it was all over.

"I know," I whispered back.

"I have a 48 hour shift." His arms wrapped around my body and drew me in closer to his chest.

I groaned. Those were the worst.

"You think you'll come into work this week?" His voice was hopeful.

"I don't think so. Probably next week." Just five more minutes, my head screamed. His chest hair was soft on my back and his arm felt right across my torso.

"Okay." Again, his mouth fell to my neck. "I'll see you in a few days then?"

My feet dragged up and down his shins.

"Yes." What kind of girl would say no to that?

Eli showered and dressed and was out the door in record time. He texted to say that the press had abandoned their post outside my door and my heartbeat slowed. Maybe it was all going to blow over. Maybe normalcy would return faster than I even expected.

The trouble with Dr. Elijah Heatherton leaving my house at 4:30 in the morning ... the newest Cincy Billionaire's house ... is that people kinda cared. And it was kind of scandalous. And despite what Eli thought of there being no press around, he was kind of wrong.

Because that morning, his picture was plastered all up in the news. Hair still slicked back from his shower. Clothes he had worn to my house the previous morning. Phone in front of him - probably scrolling through messages from the hospital. Hand shoved into one pocket on his way to his Mercedes SUV.

When they found out who he was ...

When they figured out who he had been at Emory ...

When they put it all together …

It became an even more sensational story that it had previously been.

A widower that lost a baby ... A widower that was so sad in Georgia ... A random nurse at the local hospital ... A crap ton of new money ... And they had found each other.

An unlikely romance.

I "saved" him.

He "grounded" me.

And the stories just didn't stop.

Around noon, my mom called. "Grace," her cool voice flowed through the phone. "Do you think it's time to call Megan again for some damage control?"

I couldn't tear my eyes away from the TV and I hadn't heard from Eli all morning. I cleared my throat. "Yes. I suppose it's time."

I hung up with her and texted Eli an apology. I just couldn't imagine how having his private life splashed across the media would affect him, but I knew ... I just had a feeling deep in my bones ... none of this was going to be good.

"This," she gestured around frantically, "is probably why you never answer any question about your personal life, Grace," Megan stated just so *obviously* as she sat with me at my dining room table. She had issued a stand down order to my parents and it was just her and me in this giant apartment. The dishwasher hummed gently in the background.

"Yea. Got it. What do we do?" I bit my lip and checked my phone for the hundredth time.

"Stop fidgeting. And put your phone down." She pulled out a folder - *my* folder, I presume. "We're going to release a statement. Say something like, 'We appreciate the support from the people of Cincinnati, but we're trying to regain some normalcy. We're asking for privacy, yada, yada, yada. And while Dr. Heatherton's past has been devastating, he still shines as one of Cincinnati University's best general surgeons.'"

I just stared at her. What a spin. "That's it?"

"Not much else you can do, Grace. What's done is done." She stared back.

"Okay. Release it, then." I stood to fill my coffee cup.

"Do you want me to say something about how you're planning to return to work?" Her pen was poised over a sheet of notes.

"Yes. I'm about to go crazy." I took a sip of the too hot coffee, and waited, praying for it to kick in faster than ASAP.

Megan sat at my table for another couple of hours before packing up and heading home. She wasn't very reassuring, but I was starting to understand that was her style. She was a head to head kind of girl. A meet it where it comes kind of girl. A girl that challenges the challenger. She was perfect to have in my corner.

I paced in my house. If Eli was in surgery, he would be getting out soon, or at least taking a break. He'd see my texts. He'd probably have some from friends, I'd imagine. Did he have friends? We hadn't even talked about it. He was the man that had seared my soul and I had no idea who his best friend was.

I made another pot of coffee and contemplated ordering takeout. I contemplated baking. I contemplated a Real Housewives binge. Instead, I paced with a hot cup in my hand.

He never texted me back.

I woke up the next morning restless. I opened my curtains and then shut them. Walked into the kitchen and walked back to my bedroom. I shuffled my feet and flipped through my closet. The antsy creeped up my legs, tightened my lower back, and made me grind my teeth.

I felt trapped.

I felt the walls closing in on me and had to stop in front of my bathroom mirror for a hot second. I closed my eyes and counted to twenty. I took deep breaths. I counted my deep breaths. I would conquer this.

*Fuck it*, I eventually thought. I tossed my hair into a ponytail, put on some leggings, and you know what? I charged right on out of my apartment and headed for Nordstrom's.

I found a sweet little personal shopper named Abigail and did some *damage*. Shirts and slacks and dresses and underwear and shoes and shoes and shoes and a handbag or seven and sweaters. Socks. Earrings. Fancy makeup. Pillows for my couch, cute dishrags, and a table centerpiece. Abigail and I walked through each section of the store and I just said yes.

Over and over.

Running shoes for my dad? Put it on my tab.

Perfume for my mom? Of course.

Fancy hairspray for my errant curls? Where has THAT been all my life?

Six *hours* later, and I was back in my car. My junky car that I'd had forever. It smelled like hospital food (that was probably in the backseat?) and bad choices. I chewed my lip for a second, and then I called Marshall.

"Marshall," he answered on the second ring.

"What if I want to spend more than my allotment in a month?"

He laughed. "Grace. How are you today?"

I stared out my dirty windshield. "What about a car?"

"You can afford a new car, Grace. Do you need some help today?" I could hear his smile through the phone.

I took a deep breath and felt a new mantra rise up in my belly. I needed to do this by myself. "No thanks, Marshall. I was just checking to make sure my check won't bounce."

We both chuckled at that.

"Well, call me if you need anything else."

And I hung up thinking to myself what --- what else could a girl possibly ever need? Jesus.

I drove around Cincinnati forever, it seemed like. BMW. Audi. Lexus. Ford. Chevy. I pulled into the Mercedes dealership simply because that's what I always seemed to see in the physician's parking lot at the hospital.

I settled on a Mercedes G-Class SUV. I don't know. It looked like a bunch of metal and it had red seatbelt, so I was all, "Order me one," and I think the salesman peed himself a little. In the past, buying a car had sort of been exhausting, but this time, it was anticlimactic. The beast wouldn't be in for four weeks, so I drove my shitty car back home.

When I walked through the lobby, Cleo, the door guy that needs a helluva raise, stopped me. "There's a man here to see you," he called out, as I walked by.

I stopped and raised my eyebrow at him. "Yea?"

"Yea," he said, nodding his head towards the room with the foosball table and the pool table and the refrigerator full of Shasta.

I peaked my head through and saw Eli staring at an abstract piece of art on the wall. "Pretend like you've never seen me," I muttered to Cleo.

After not having heard from Eli for a solid 48 hours? Well. I could go another 12. And my bed sounded oh-so-good ... no matter how good he looked in his sweater and khaki pants.

My mom called in the morning and when I figured out what even was happening, I realized there was something stuck to my face. It was part of an Oreo wrapper and listen - I have no shame. I'm not sad one bit about having eaten a whole row of Oreos while thinking of The Good Doctor awaiting my return in the lobby.

"Gracie? How are you? Do you want dad and I to come up today and hang out?" My mom sounded worried. Since That Spring When Everything Happened, she's sounded worried a billion times. For awhile there, I was concerned that it was her only operating level, but since then, I've realized that she is ... in fact ... just a mom. And, turns out, that's just what moms do.

I took a deep breath. "Sure? What are you guys doing today?" I figured this afternoon, I'd call the hospital and ask them to start scheduling me.

"It's Sunday, dear."

Shit. Weekly Family Dinner.

"No, no. I'll come to see you guys." I sat up in bed and readied myself. "Just give me a half hour." Who knew? Days on the calendar flew by and I had no idea what day it even was.

"See you soon, then. Love you." She hung up and I flew - and I do mean *flew* into action. I tugged on some pretty fancy new leggings and tried on a few of my new sweaters before I found the one that I liked the best. My shower felt amazing and not one time - *not one time* - did I think of Elijah Heatherton.

Mom had meatloaf in the oven and was snapping peas when I walked in. "Your dad's in the study. Go say hello," she said without even turning around. I didn't think it was even odd, considering I hadn't even realized it was Sunday.

I shoved open dad's study before even knocking because *Sunday*. And *family dinner*. And *I was family*. And also? *I'm an only child*. I didn't even think that - you know - someone *else* might be invited to Sunday dinner.

Jesus.

*I was wrong.*

And can we just stop and talk for a second about how fast my mother's switch flipped? Because? Well. Now she must be all kinds of …

"Eli. Hi." Elijah Heatherton. My mother must be all kinds of Team Elijah Heatherton.

He turned from my dad's shelf of very good scotch and nodded at me. He freaking *nodded* at me like some kind of Darcy Incarnate. He was in my dad's flipping study - the study that I'd spent countless days in and all he had for me was a nod.

Listen. Never mind me just leaving him or whatever in the lobby of my apartment building. This was diff.

He was in my family home.

And a nod

"Hey, daddy." Dad walked over to me and gave me a solid hug.

"Gracie. Glad you could join us today. Your friend here, Dr. Heatherton, also decided to join us." He sat down at the game table that occupied the majority of the room. "You wanna play a game of chess? You need a drink?"

I looked from my dad to Eli and then back to my dad again. "Uhm. No thanks. I think I'll ask mom if she needs any help." As quickly and err... as "gracefully" as I could, I exited stage left and found some kind of weird solace in the kitchen.

"Mom. Eli is in the study with dad." I picked up the bag of lettuce and began to cut it open.

"Yes. I know. I invited him. But that was before ..." She trailed off. VERY UNLIKE MOM BEHAVIOR.

***** Pro Tip: If moms ever "trail off"? Don't prod. Leave 'em be. Chances are? They're about to teach you a lesson you don't want to hear or already know or both. But …**

"Before ..." I prodded. I couldn't help myself. Dang it!

"Before I knew about whether or not you both were still a thing. He seemed just so surprised when I invited him because *apparently* you avoided him last night in your lobby. He saw you, Grace Morgan. He saw you walk away and have the doorman take care of your baggage and you know what? *He still showed up*." She paused here to take a breath and thank God.

"So of course I invited him. Of course I did. Imagine my surprise at my own daughter behaving so poorly."

I could feel her eyes on me.

"Mom. He didn't respond one time to me after the news broke of him and his wife and his baby at Emory." I added croutons to the salad.

"So?" She leaned up against the island. "Does that give you any kind of leave to act so cold?" She studied me and I didn't really love it.

"No." I sighed. "I just. I just didn't like how he ignored me for two days. I needed ..." I waved my arms around frantically. What *did* I need? A drink? *Yes*. "I needed him. *Something* from him. Some kind of check in and one never came." I started washing lettuce with gusto in the sink. It was the sex. The sex made me expect more from him.

Out of the corner of my eye, I saw my mom shrug her damn shoulders and I almost threw the head of lettuce I was holding at her, but -

"I came to see if I could help with anything."

Of course Eli had been standing there the whole friggin' time.

"I think Grace might need some help putting that salad together. I'm going to check on Morg." My mother *breezed* out of the kitchen and no thank you, Caroline Morgan, I certainly DO NOT need help with this salad.

I felt him behind me and I leaned my head back into his chest without even realizing what I was doing. I was exasperated, but really, I just wanted him. To know he was there. To feel him. Behind me literally *and* figuratively.

His mouth was next to my ear and his chin stubble dragged along my neck. "I'm here," he whispered.

And fuck it all, I cried. Giant, sloppy tears fell down my cheeks and we'd only been out on like three dates, but here I was crying at my mother's sink ... because why?

His hands were warm on my arms as he stood sentry behind me. As he stood behind me and let me lose it. As he stood behind me. "I'm right here," he whispered again.

And that's when I realized that my tears were full of gratitude. Full of sweet relief.

He was here, now.

And that was enough.

After an uneventful Sunday dinner, he followed me back to my apartment, and the whole way home ... I could feel it. A conversation was coming. A long, complicated, "This is what we do from now on," conversation. I was tired just thinking about it.

We rode up the elevator in silence. His thumb tracked across my back and it was more comforting than any words he could've said. I closed my eyes and took deep breaths.

- *Billionaire Captures Widow*
- *Cincy's Most Eligible Bachelorette Already Off the Market?*
- *Widow Finds Love with Billionaire*
- *Widow, Widow, Widow*
- *Billionaire, Billionaire, Billionaire*

My life flashed before my eyes as the elevator carried us towards my penthouse apartment. News headlines and shared Facebook articles from "friends" all swirled around my head. Where do we even start? I wondered. Where do we even start?

I unlocked my apartment door and let us in. I tossed my jacket on the couch and opened my wine refrigerator (because yes, I have one, and yes, it has a few bottles of $3 Trader Joe's wine, don't judge me). I poured a tall glass and he just waited, leaning up against the counter.

"You didn't say a word." I stared down at my drink. "Not one thing. For two days. Not a word."

He nodded his head. He pushed himself off of the white quartz countertop and headed over to me. Brushing my hair off of my shoulder, his hands fell down my arms. "This is going to be heavy."

I turned my body and looked up at him. "I can handle heavy." I mean, I could, right? Just for good measure, I took a solid, deep, restorative breath in.

"After Sarah ..." He trailed off and I wondered if the word *Sarah* was always going to hurt him when he spoke it. "After Sarah, I never imagined I would ever find someone else again." He looked at me finally. He looked at me like he was seeing me for the first time. "I never imagined I'd find someone like you." His eyes followed my hair down to my shoulder and across my collar bone. Heat rose in my cheeks.

"But here you are." His eyes finally met mine again. "Here you are and you're beautiful. And funny. And smart. And I started to think that I could find my life again with you." His fingers tightened in mine.

His fingers tightened and all I could think about was his words were in past tense.

"I came out of a splenectomy and my phone was actually one fire. People I hadn't spoken to since med school were hounding me for information." He shook his head and looked at the ceiling and gulped *my* wine. "And they all said the same thing." He cleared his throat. "It's about time you've moved on."

And just ... ouch. I'll admit that one kind of stung a little. He looked like some kind of wounded rabbit and I wanted to feel sorry for him, but I was also a little wounded.

His hands rubbed the back of his neck. "I took two days. Two days to wonder and decide whether or not I was truly over her loss." His eyes found mine again and I wondered.

Was he really over her? Over her loss? Over what they could've had?

His hands found mine again. "I'll always love her and the baby, Grace. I'll always love what we had. Cherish it. Respect it. But that doesn't mean I'm not ready to move forward." He kissed my forehead, and then my nose. And then my lips. "Forward with you." His tongue licked at my bottom lip, and he whispered, "If you'll still have me."

And I ask you, what girl would say no?

It was slow that night, too. Slow, soft. An exploration. His hands felt like they were all over me. My hair. My thighs. My wrists. My ankles. And I gave myself freely to him because I realized that to move forward? The only way was together.

You might think it's crazy. You do, don't you? You think it's nuts? After only a few "dates", I'm all in with a man I hardly know? Well, maybe. But -

I just don't think life is meant to be lived in the halfway.

It was a Monday. Eli was in my bed sleeping off a weekend of on call duty, and I was standing in my closet looking at my carefully folded scrubs. Somewhere in the melee, we decided that I'd go to work for the first day without him. That he'd stay back, and I would go it alone. Now, here in my closet, I was wondering if that was the best decision.

I pulled a pair of navy scrub pants from the stack, and quickly dressed. I was pouring a cup of coffee when he finally decided to join me in the living room.

**Side Note: That man? In his boxer briefs and his tan abs and his messy hair? Sweet baby Jesus, there would just never be anyone else that will ever compare. That's all.**

"Are you ready for today?" He poured himself a cup and took a deep, heavy, sleepy breath in. He was exhausted - physically and emotionally. A patient had died on him the night before, and I was sure he'd carry it with him for weeks to come.

"I think so." From what I'd heard from mom and Eli, things had *somewhat* died down at the hospital in the two weeks since I'd been gone. I was praying, praying, praying for a quiet day.

He nodded at me. "Call me if you need to?" His imploring eyes found mine and I spent the rest of my precious minutes before work making out with the hottest doctor in Ohio.

I walked to my car and I wondered if it would always be like it was right now. Would I always kiss him goodbye? Would he always have coffee with me in the kitchen, find my hand, and press his warm palm into mine? Would he always tell me to have a good day?

Deep in my belly. Deep down inside of me, I felt it. I felt that glimmer of hope. I felt it bubbling up through my throat and I knew without a doubt - *without a doubt* - I knew I'd do anything in my power to keep him in my life.

I tossed my stuff into my neglected locker, put on my ID badge, and readied myself. As I walked to the nurse's station, I took deep, sustaining breaths. And a prayer I had been praying for weeks lifted up through my chest. *Lord, help me make it through today.*

"Grace Morgan! Hi!" Tammy. Tammy? I think it was Tammy, was the first to say hello. And Tammy was definitely not a general surgery nurse. Tammy was definitely an oncology nurse. But Tammy was definitely standing here in front of me on the wrong floor.

"Hi." I smiled sweetly, and took a seat behind the desk. "Tabitha," I called over to my old friend. "Fill me in, girl." I made serious eye contact with the director of nursing for our floor and she scooted her chair over to me. Taking pity on me, I suppose? She carried over four charts, and that's how the first thirty minutes of my shift went. Tammy? Tammy. Definitely Tammy faded away.

After briefing me on the patients we had on our floor and the surgeries I was scheduled for that day, I could feel the question on her lips. I looked over at her. "I'm sorry I couldn't tell you." I shrugged my shoulders.

She peered over at me. "I don't care about the money. But Dr. Heatherton. You be careful with him."

I was taken aback. "Of course." That was the first thing that came into my head. Why would I NOT take care of the god that was currently sleeping in my bed?

She rolled her chair away and I stared after her. "He's a wonderful man," I called to her.

"I know," she said, as she continued her charting.

Slowly, I turned back to my own charts. So strange. I filed it away and vowed to ask Eli about her when I got back home. Would he be there waiting for me? At *home*? Such a strange notion ... that *home* would be with Eli after only a few weeks.

I checked on my patients, charted a few things, and was on my way to get Mr. Roberts in 1302 a warmed blanket when I was accosted by Jared - another nurse on my floor.

"Saw your press conference, Grace." He smiled at me. He had always been genial, but there was a definite question in his voice. Would I always feel like this? Would I always feel like someone was asking me for something?

"Yeah. It was a pretty crazy couple of days. How are you? How's your mom?" Jared's mom had some sort of kidney issue, but he was pretty tight-lipped about it. Every now and then, he took the day off to help her to appointments. He'd even consulted with Eli a couple of times about care.

He looked down. "She's good," he nodded, and then finally looked up at me. "Getting stronger every day."

The towel I held in my hand had now cooled, thus defeating the purpose of even grabbing one from the warmer. "Well, I'll see you around, okay? I need to go look after Mr. Roberts." I smiled again at him and we awkwardly shuffled past each other.

*Lord, help me make it through the day*, I prayed again. *Help me make it through the dang day.*

I had one surgery on my schedule for the day and it was an hour-long appendectomy with Dr. Hall. He was pretty jovial, and everyone loved him. I smiled as I scrubbed in. This was the last thing standing between me and the door and Eli.

Music was already on as I stepped in the operating room, and the patient was being wheeled in. As per usual, Dr. Hall walked in with a blaze of good humor and jokes. I set up next to him, ready to assist. Dr. Hall didn't disappoint. In his booming voice, he announced to the operating room that we had a VERY SPECIAL GUEST among us, and I felt my cheeks go hot. He continued, "I'm sure you've heard the news lately, but I just wanted to make sure that we all are on board here - there will be no hounding, there will be no joking, and there will be no whispers behind backs." My eyes slid to my right, and his laughing eyes were looking not at me, but -

"Maggie here," he motioned to the nurse standing in front of him, "is engaged!" Laughter and polite clapping filled the room. "And," he continued almost to himself, "The Cincy Billionaire just handed me lap pads ... which is something I never thought I'd get to say."

Again laughter.

And a piece of whatever heavy, hot thing that had been on my chest for weeks -

A piece of that lifted.

Work was much the same for the ensuing days. People were polite, reserved, and stood back. Mom and I had lunch a few times in the cafeteria, and we ignored the strange looks. I suppose when you've won a billion dollars, one would think cafeteria food wouldn't be on your agenda. But? I kind of liked their macaroni and cheese.

Tabitha continued to side-eye me, and she watched diligently every single time Eli approached.

Jared continued to study me.

The only place, thank goodness, where I felt money didn't follow me was the operating room. There, as it turned out, it didn't matter how much money you had. And it was a Thursday - a rainy Thursday when a man in his fifties came in. A routine procedure went south.

Wildly south.

And the man on the table with greying hair that looked an awful lot like my dad's was suddenly in distress.

And I suppose this happens from time to time.

The operating room turned into a flurry of activity.

Dr. Hall started immediate compressions.

Paddles were readied.

Monitors went berserk.

The hum of talking - exacerbated by the seriousness of the situation - was drowned out by the barking of Dr. Hall.

"Come on," he kept yelling. "Come. ON." I handed him paddles. And his booming voice filled the small room. "CLEAR." Automatically, my hands went in the air. The body on the table jerked.

Compressions again.

Vitals called out over the commotion.

Paddles again.

Charged again.

Clear.

Again.

And again.

And then, someone's terrified voice. "He's back. We've got a rhythm."

I sighed heavily. I hadn't even realized I was holding my breath.

I looked down at our patient and his face was so serene. He had a scar next to his lips. Had he cut himself shaving when he was a kid? When I prepped him for surgery, he took off a wedding ring and the indentation stayed behind.

It was here - the moment I was walking to my car in the dull rain - right here. This day when I was acutely aware of how fragile life really is. In that moment, I knew I was being followed. Watched. My breath stuttered in my chest and my steps quickened. I held my keys like some kind of weapon, and I nearly ran to my car.

The feeling of being watched? Followed? That feeling would follow me for weeks, but I would chalk it up to being insecure with my new "fame".

I was so wrong.

## Lesson #7

**Judgement: The ability to make considered decisions, or come to sensible conclusions**

**Against his better judgement, Lawson scheduled an interview.**

When the newspaper called him, I assume he jumped at the chance. A boy like Lawson - no real job, no real family, no real ambition? A boy like him could be easily swayed. I should've seen it coming a mile away, and had I told Megan Rhodes, my PR person, about him - she probably would've. Maybe she would've gotten to him first? Who knows?

The damage was done.

Sunday afternoon, while Eli and I were having an easy dinner with my parents, Lawson was sitting down with a shady reporter in the south of Cincinnati. He would drink bad coffee and smirk in front of the tape recorder.

The lies would pour from his mouth and my mother wouldn't look at me the same for weeks.

Drugs.

Sex.

More drugs.

More sex.

I've never even smoke marijuana, but suddenly everyone at the hospital was looking at my arms, examining my face, wondering how I kept my heroin addiction a secret for so long.

Megan did as much damage control as she possibly could, and Sean went hard at Lawson for slander. My drug tests from the hospital came back clean, hair follicle samples were offered to anyone that would listen, but the damage was already one.

Cincinnati's darling lottery winner that everyone was rooting for?

Well, it was easier to believe that she just might be a whore.

*[...] and she didn't care where it came from, or who was dealing it to her, she would toss out the money from her pocket and walk away with coke, meth, or marijuana. It didn't matter to her.*

*[...] Yea, I suppose I've given her money for sex. Didn't matter, though. She'd just take the money to a dealer. I kinda stopped doing it, ya know? I didn't want to feed that habit. I didn't want to have to tell her mother that I was the reason she was dead - because I gave her money for a bad job, and then she blew it on drugs.*

*[...] Was I the only one? I don't know. I doubt it. She isn't the type of girl that just has one guy, you know what I mean? Everyone wants a piece of Grace Morgan, you know what I mean?*

*[...] I used to tell her, "Grace, baby, you can't go to the hospital like this today. You have patients. These people depend on you to treat them. You can't go in high."*

*[...] I don't know, you know? I don't know if her superiors know. You should ask them - you should definitely check into that. I can't imagine they'd want to keep her there if she's stealing the drugs from the people she's trying to help.*

Eli, for what it's worth, took it all in stride. He went to the hospital to do one thing - and that was care for patients. He had never been overly friendly before, and this only made him even more closed off. He came by my apartment whenever he wasn't working, and we ate dinner together - high above it all.

I contemplated quitting my job.

Megan continued to work.

Sean continued to push.

Eventually, it was Lawson caught on the street corner selling drugs. And like these things do, the ebb and the flow, the press was back on my side. Megan went after him like the pit bull I pay her to be and the world started to right itself again.

The more I think about it, though, I imagine this is how Sadie found Lawson. Between his tell all to the papers, and then his drug charge, I'm quite certain that he was easy to track down for someone looking hard. I wouldn't put it together for months. But it was there, tucked away neatly behind shiny headlines and monotonous days at work.

Sadie Traverty was at work.

The Ohio winter passed quietly. Eli and I developed some kind of relationship that felt good and true and right and fulfilling.

We found ourselves on quiet streets, hand in hand, talking about where we were going to be in five years. Or ten.

We found ourselves entwined under expensive sheets during long afternoons.

I told him everything about Sadie. He told me everything about Sarah. Together, we learned each other. He had a scar on his hip from a boating accident. I had a scar on my eyebrow from a car wreck. His mother spoke fluent Portuguese, and his dad was a doctor in New York. My dad enjoyed golfing with him occasionally, and my mom made his favorite dessert.

We were forging our lives together. Forward.

We talked about vacationing together and we talked about moving in together. Small steps. Big steps. Timidly and wildly. We talked about it all.

We decided to set up a foundation in Sarah's name benefitting infant loss and my mother took the challenge head on. I've never seen her work with such consuming ferocity, and before we even knew it, Sarah's Faith was off the ground and running. Named after both his first wife and the baby that Sadie killed in her bathroom, the foundation was aimed at helping parents work through tragedy and grief. It felt right. And time and time again, Eli and I were fulfilled with the knowledge that the people in our lives were carrying forward names that *mattered.*

For the most part, things were as normal as they would ever be. I shopped for my mom's birthday without worry, and I splurged on regular spa visits. Quietly, I helped Jared's mother with her medical expenses, and watched with joy as the dark circles under his eyes dissipated. We were all starting to find our groove.

I would look back on this time later in my life and feel like it had shadows of yellow. The same color of yellow that swept across the sky in the mornings when Eli had to go to the hospital, and the same color of yellow that whispered to us to head for bed in the evenings. The yellow flecks in Eli's irises. I would look back on this time later in my life and call it the most perfect few months that I had ever encountered.

I wonder sometimes why I never felt like something big was coming. I wonder sometimes why I felt so settled and assured. Was it because of Sean and

Megan and Marshall and Eli? Was it because of the money? Why wasn't my intuition triggered?

Or maybe, just maybe - I believed that I'd already lived the worst days of my life. Maybe I believed in happily ever afters just a little too hard. Maybe, I thought the afternoon at Sadie's house, and the newspaper article, and the feelings of being kept hostage in my apartment were enough for one life.

Or maybe I was just oblivious.

• The first time I realized something might be wrong - and I've thought about this a lot. I have contemplated for months now, and I have come to this one very distinct moment. *This* moment, this day? This is the day that our courses all veered.

I was sitting at my desk at the nurse's station on our General Surgery floor. I had charts out in front of me and a half-eaten granola bar in my hand. It was almost the end of my shift. I was desperately looking forward to a hot bath when I got home.

I smelled him before I saw him and goosebumps raised all over my arms. Smiling, I looked up. "Where have you been all day, handsome?" But my smile fell the moment I saw his face. He wasn't in scrubs, though he was supposed to work that day. He peered at me. "What's wrong, Eli?" My own eyebrows furrowed in fear. He had a nice suit on, no tie, and his hands were shoved in his pockets.

He only shook his head. "I'm not working the rest of the week. Can you push my surgeries? Or ask Dr. Hall? I'll speak with my patients." He nodded his head one time at me and clenched his jaw.

And then he left.

And I am *certain* my mouth hung open.

I pushed the surgeries I could, and I shuffled Dr. Hall's schedule to accommodate the others. I pumped anyone and everyone for information, but all I received in return were shoulder shrugs.

And because Eli is *Eli* and he does and does and does for other people, no one really had any problems covering for him.

After work that night, I headed straight to his house. Using the key he gave me at Christmas, I unlocked the front door. "Eli?" I called out. I flipped on the foyer light and then the hall light. "Are you home?" I didn't even think about checking the garage or calling first. Then the kitchen light.

I trekked all through the house and realized he wasn't there. Everything was in perfect order - even his mail was neatly lined up on the counter. I pulled out my phone before I left.

**Hey. Just wondering where you're at. Dinner?**

I shoved it back into my pocket, turned off all of the lights at his house, locked the door back up and left. When I got back to my own apartment, it felt cooler. Different. For the first time in a very long time, Eli wasn't there. I sort of glanced around at the couch and kitchen and dining room table. I didn't know really what to do with myself.

**I've got some things to take care of. I'm out of town - be back Friday. Talk soon.**

I stared at my phone.
Legitimately stared.
Willed more words to appear.
Out of town? Who in the hell goes out of town just like that?
And what things? What was he taking care of?
And for the love of all that was holy, why didn't he mention any of this to me before he left?

While I was walking throughout my empty apartment, Eli was stumbling through a cold cemetery in Georgia. The ground was hard beneath his brown dress shoes. His grey overcoat matched the weather, and his hardened eyes were set across the tombstones - on a small corner under a large magnolia tree.

Later - much later - he would tell me of how the frozen grass crunched under his soles, and how the bench in front of his first wife's grave felt like ice as he sat down. His leather gloved hands rubbed together, his ears pink from the wind, and the tombstone sparkling. Her name, and a picture of her smiling face stared right back at him. Baby Heatherton was chiseled under her name.

Baby Heatherton.
Baby.
His baby.

His head dropped, and he spoke to her low and steady. The words he whispered over a grave he never thought would be are the words that I'll never get to know. I can only surmise that he talked to her about me. That he told her he'd met someone. That he told her about my life, and that he also told her about Sadie Traverty. Because by this time?

The Sadie Effect was in full swing.

I wish I would've known that he was suffering, and I wish he would've asked me to go with him.

Instead, my Eli walked to Sarah's tombstone, and ran his fingers over its rough top. He would visit her parents next. He would sit in the living room that Sarah grew up in, and he would tell her parents about me, too. He would drink warm coffee with a still grieving mother. He would talk shop with a clearly distressed father. He would sit in a chair and he would still feel the heavy sorrow that pressed down on his shoulders.

And then he would ask about the letters.

## Lesson #8

**Letter: A written, typed, or printed communication, especially one sent in an envelope by mail or messenger.**

**And the letters began to come, and they were signed by Sarah. His Sarah.**

Eli had been staying at my apartment for much of those golden months. And every time he went back to his own house, he checked the mail. Each time, there was a letter. Addressed to Eli in a swirling font, the letters carried Sarah's home return address.

The first time he received one, I wonder if it buckled him. I wonder if his breath caught in his throat like some kind of angry wildfire. I wonder if he fell to his knees. And I wonder why he didn't say a word.

Like clockwork, the letters came every Monday for two months. I imagine he tore through them, desperate, starved. I imagine he ripped open the envelopes and let her words seep into his skin. I imagine he stared at her signature and wondered how his Sarah -

The same Sarah that died on a cold, rainy Georgia day.
The same Sarah with her grandmother's wedding ring on her fourth finger.
The same Sarah that was carrying a child with Heatherton genes, and the same Sarah that he had sought comfort in time and time again.

I imagine he stared at her signature and wondered how his Sarah was communicating with him.

When he sat in her living room with her parents, his coat hanging in the hallway like it had a thousand times before - for Thanksgivings and Christmases and family dinners - he probably hunched over his knees. His elbows probably dug into his legs. I've seen him do it a thousand times while he was in deep thought.

I wonder how his words must have sounded to her parents. And when he pulled the typed letters from his pocket, I wonder how they must've felt. The crushing hope that probably ignited deep in their tummies. I wonder if they felt that.

Months later, Eli would describe to me how Sarah's mother handled the letters. How gentle her touch was, how her fingers stroked over the words, how her sobs shook her too-small frame. He would describe her father, ashen at seeing her familiar signature at the bottom. He would describe how her dad stood at the mantle, his arms bracing himself, and his head sinking down low.

Her mother would read the words out loud to a quiet room.

*Do you miss me, Elijah? Do you miss my touch in the morning? Do you miss feeling our baby kick at night? Do you miss my cold toes on your calves and waking up together? I miss you so much that I ache for you.*

*Elijah, can you hear me at night? I call out to you, but I can never find you. Can you come to me? Are you out there, still? I miss you so much that I cannot bear it.*

*It's so cold where I am, Elijah. I can never seem to catch my breath and I'm worried. I need you so much. It's like I can almost feel you if I reach out far enough and close my eyes tight enough. Hurry up, Eli. Hurry up.*

Together, the three of them would muse for hours. The sun would set, and Eli would nurse a Jameson. The ice would melt. His glass cooled his heated forehead, and his collar - long unbuttoned - still felt tight on his neck.

*Hurry up, Eli. Hurry up.*

Those words, though. Those words would rest on his chest for months.

Back in Cincinnati, I cleaned up my already clean kitchen. I poured myself a large glass of red wine. I put on yoga pants and a huge sweater. I curled up on my couch and turned on some music. I scrolled through my phone - willing it to ding with an incoming message from Eli.

One, of course, would never come.

Restless, I stood from the couch, drained my glass, and went to bed. With the morning, new mercies would come, I told myself. In the morning, I'd look at all of this with a fresh set of eyes.

It wouldn't matter, as it turns out. I awoke the next morning with the same unease in the pit of my stomach. I still hadn't heard from Eli, and I still felt some sort of weird chill in the air. It was the chill of the unknown, and I didn't like it. I called my mom.

“Why don’t you come on over?” My mom’s voice was laced with the kind of concern that I hadn’t heard in awhile. The kind of concern that I’d grown accustomed to during The Sadie Mess.

“I think I will. Is dad home, too?” I searched through my closet for a pair of sweats, and was dressed in no time.

“Yep! I’ll make us a nice afternoon snack.” My momma. Killing whatever ails me with food. I don’t hate that about her.

I pulled into the familiar drive of my parent’s house, and put my SUV in park. Spring was coming, but February in Ohio was still cold. My scarf came up to my chin and my gloved hands rested on the steering wheel.

How many times had I rushed to my parent’s house for comfort? How many times had my mother baked cinnamon rolls for an afternoon snack? How many times would I have to do this?

My foot hit the cement driveway, and I was so caught up in myself that I didn’t even notice the familiar junky car at the end of the street. I didn’t even notice the familiar profile of Lawson. I just ... didn’t even notice.

I never, ever notice.

Mom answered the door in her slippers, and pulled me close. “I saved the frosting for you,” she whispered in my ear. And that’s how I spent my afternoon. Mom, dad, and me. Together at the kitchen table playing a rousing game of Scrabble, and hours passed. Mom made a quick dinner, and we still sat together. A trio forged in a fire from ten years ago, and still - they save me.

It was dark when I finally decided to go home. Mom, for what it was worth, tried her best to coerce me into staying in my old bedroom. I had to work in the morning; otherwise, I would’ve easily said yes. There wasn’t much about my apartment that seemed to be very appealing.

We said our goodbyes at the door and they stood sentry, watching me – probably until I was just a dot down the street. When the lights flashed as my car unlocked, I noticed a small piece of paper on my windshield wipers. I pulled it off, assuming it was an ad for a local pizza place. Mildly surprised, I read the words, “Got Faith?”

You guys.
I *know* how dumb I sound right now.

I know that you’re going to think I should’ve seen ALL of this coming about a billion (get it?) miles an hour, but I didn’t. Instead, I thought the small scrap of paper was left behind by some kind of weird religious zealots, and I tossed it into my parent's garbage container. I waved again at my parents in the doorway, and I just -

*I didn't think about it again.*

At home, I sent Eli a quick message.

**Thinking of you. How are you today?**

And then, I drew a hot bath, dumped in some bubbles, and slid in. Jazz echoed up softly from the speakers throughout the apartment, and my eyes closed. The unrest that had abated at mom and dad's swift returned with the dark apartment and the twinkling lights below my fortress. The heat from the water soaked into my body and my shoulders relaxed a little.

On the vanity, my phone buzzed, and I prayed it was Eli. Instead, I would later be disappointed to see that it was my mom checking to make sure I'd made it home okay, and then again when the doorman texted to tell me that my Chinese food had been delivered.

I sat at my kitchen table, ate my dinner with every single light on, and checked over Sarah's Faith documents. My eyes grew tired, and I gave up work around midnight. Sleep would come much later, and it was fitful.

I dreamed of creek beds.

At work the next day, I realized I'd passed the line of worry and I was straight into the area labeled "Pissed Off". I slammed my charts on a nearby desk, my pen dug into the paper, my glasses (definitely NOT masking my tired eyes) slid down my nose, and my lip hurt under the pressure of my teeth.

"Grace?" Tabitha called out to me from the nurse's station.

I looked over at her. I raised my eyebrows and shrugged at her. "What?"

She furrowed that mom-brow at me, and beckoned me over. And listen. Tabitha? Not someone you ignore.

I stepped behind the large rounded desk, and (nicely) put my charts down. "What?" I asked again.

"Sit with me and work on those." She turned her chair back around to her computer and didn't say another word.

I stood for a second and looked round. Eventually, I sat as she commanded me to.

"He'll be back," she called over her shoulder. "Stop pouting. He's coming back." I could hear her fingernails tap the keys behind me.

Begrudgingly, and a bit pissy that she could tell so easily what had me so sour, I opened a chart. "How do *you* know?" I uncapped my pen. Noting the time, I jotted down a few numbers.

"Because he just called and said he'd be back to work tomorrow." With that, I could hear her chair roll back and she was gone. Down the hall she went, and my questions were only left to the empty air around me.

*Tomorrow*? So he could call *Tabitha*? But he couldn't friggin' pick up his cell phone long enough to text me that he was still alive?

And that's when I moved from the land of "Pissed Off" to the land of "Raging Hot Mad".

The day would prove to be a trying one, and that would be the last time I genuinely had time to focus on Eli. A complicated surgery came next, a patient and his family after that, and then a patient who needed someone - *anyone* - to talk to for a while. I sat on a plastic chair in the corner of a cold room, and listened to cat stories, stories about the war, grand-momma's chicken salad memories, and how the Yankees just might pull it off this year. I laughed in the right spots, reached for his hand in the right spots, and eventually, finally, blessedly, he slept.

• Random Grace Note: Sometimes, people just need someone to talk to. I think that the world's problems would be mostly solved if we just learned to listen. And I don't mean listening to just respond - I mean listening, hearing, and letting the words and perspectives sift down into you. There's something about being a nurse that has taught me to really sit in the moment, and to really take in what another person is saying to me.

I left that room completely exhausted. The week had been a doozy. How many days had Eli been gone? Three? Four? I walked to my car, my keys out, and my head on a swivel. It was always unnerving to walk in the parking lot at night, and this time was no different. I always got about halfway to my car before I regretted not asking for a security guard to escort me. One day, I'd learn my lesson. But today wasn't that day.

I climbed in, started my car, and immediately turned on the heated seats. I was tired of being cold, and I was tired of thinking of Eli. How had my life come to revolve around him so quickly? How had I let all of my walls down? The small resistance I had to men had promptly flown out the proverbial window, and here I was - left to trod after him.

And I was angry.

I thought what we had been building was this good and perfect thing, and I thought we were both on the same page and that page really is just -

You don't leave.
Ever.

You don't pick up and leave someone that you're building a together thing with, and you don't just go radio silent on them in the middle.

You don't abandon.

And in the end, that's how I felt. I felt abandoned. Closed out. And I didn't even know what was going on.

I pulled into my garage and immediately noticed Eli's SUV parked in the visitor spot. I let my engine idle for a second before putting it in reverse. Running away sure seemed like a good idea. Even though for the last three days, the only thing I've really wanted was him.

Listen. On the List of People that Make Perfect Sense, you will never find my name.

I went through the Starbucks drive through and ordered us both a drink because you know just as well as I do that I wouldn't be able to stay away. And eventually, my curiosity won out and I headed back. I parked in my labeled spot, pulled out my keys, and headed into the building.

Never - not one time - did I ever believe my building wasn't secure. It was well lit. There was a gated entry with a 24-hour guard. I didn't even glance over my shoulder.

My door was unlocked. The lights were low, and Eli was standing at the floor to ceiling living room windows. His suit jacket was laying on the couch, and the back of his hair was even mussed. He turned when he heard the door shut behind me.

"Hey," he leaned back against the window frame.

I moved to the kitchen, my footsteps heavy, my coat constricting, and the coffee in my hands hot. I put the cups down, and tossed my purse onto the counter. "Hi." I couldn't look at him because the second I did, I'd be all over him. Instead, I hung my keys on the hook, and shuffled through the mail.

"I'm sorry." His voice quaked, and that's what made my head snap up. In the lamplight, his cheeks were glistening.

And I went to him.

You would've, too.

His arms clutched me to his warm body, and I melted into him.

He sniffed in my ear. "I missed you." His hands dragged through my hair as he clung to me. I realized it just then - he needed me just as much as I needed him.

And damn if that wasn't restorative.

I sighed, and a week's worth of frustration came out with it. "You've got some things to explain."

He nodded into my neck. "In a second." He breathed me in, and pulled me even closer to him. "In a second," he whispered again.

We stood holding each other for long minutes. My hand rubbed up and down the back of his blue checked dress shirt, and his fingers brushing through my hair. We swayed to music neither of us could hear, and my eyes closed.

"I went to see Sarah's parents." His warm palms left my back and my hair and the cool air that replaced them was mostly devastating. He took my hands and led me to the couch. Together, we curled up under a blanket.

I blinked at him. I let his fingers move methodically over mine. I watched as his eyes fixated on the clock above my stove. I didn't speak. The seconds ticked, and he still didn't speak. Just when I was about to get up and grab our drinks from the counter - and just when I was about to badger him.

He cleared his throat.

"Their living room hasn't changed a bit. But they've just ... *aged*. Both of them. And they look so ... small." He has such long lashes. Every time he blinks, they slap at his cheeks. "They weren't surprised to see me. I thought they would be." His voice was halting. Haunted. "I thought they'd be surprised." The word felt like they were tearing at his throat.

His hands had turned cold, and I slowly inched them out of his reach. This was not *my* Eli. This was *Sarah's* Eli.

"We sat together for hours that first day, and the sun went down, and her picture was still on the mantle, and I sat in the same rocking chair." He trailed off.

*The first day?* He was with them for more than one day? "Why did you go see them?" My own voice sounded tired.

"I thought they might know already." He cleared his voice.

"About what? Eli? That they might know about what?" I was so confused and he was so far away.

He stood up to pace. "The letters are signed the same way that she signed her own name. The S is hard, and the H at the end has a loop that crosses under her name. She signed it that way since grade school." His hands were in his pockets. He was staring back at the Cincy skyline. "A thousand people have probably seen her sign things that way. It could be anyone."

Shit. He could've been talking in code, for all I knew.

"What the *hell* are you talking about?"

"I've been getting letters from Sarah." He spoke to the window and his voice was soft and you could've knocked me over with a feather.

"I'm sorry?" You guys. I had so many questions that I didn't even know where to start. She was still alive? Then who died in the accident? Who did they bury? *Where was his baby?*

"I know it's crazy," he rattled keys in his pockets. "But every Monday, I get a letter and it has her parent's address on the envelope and it's got her name signed and she's dead." He cleared his throat. "I know she's dead."

I just blinked. And blinked.

"So, I went to see her parents to see if they were getting them, too. Or if it was them sending the letters. Or if they *knew* who was sending them." He shook his head, and still wouldn't turn from the windows. "They're just so ... cruel. I don't even know who would do such a thing."

Letters from your dead wife showing up weekly?

Yea. I can see why he went off the deep end.

I cleared my throat. "What did her parents say?"

"They were so confused. And so hurt." He finally turned. "I just keep causing them more and more pain." He sat down next to me and I was stunned.

"You think Sarah's death was your fault?" I stared at him, incredulous. There were a lot of layers here, okay? I went to the "easiest" one first.

He turned his head to look at me and that's when I realized we had taken an immeasurable amount of steps backwards. My Eli was still Sarah's Eli. Instead of an attentive and loving boyfriend, he was again a grieving widow in the throes of pain. It was as if no time had passed at all. I reached my hand up to his cheek and his flinch broke me a little inside.

"She never would've been out on that damn road if it hadn't been for me." Abruptly, he stood. "I'm going to head home, shower, and go into the hospital. I'm so behind and I've got patients." He grabbed his jacket, and was at the door before I could even say goodbye.

## Lesson #9

**Hostage: A person seized or held as security for the fulfillment of a condition**

**And just like that, I was a mother f'ing hostage.**

Is it cliche to say that it started off like any other day? Is it cliche to say that I was wearing my favorite sweatpants, and my softest t-shirt, and it was a typical Sunday? How about if I tell you that things were sort of getting back to a "new" normal? Or that I was having a good hair day?

Eli slowly - and I do mean *slowly* - regained footing. My guess is that he started utilizing a counselor, but he never mentioned it. Eventually, we worked our way back into a new flow, and talk of the letters was put on the back burner for a hot sec. I thought that, once Eli had a chance to just ... *take a minute,* we'd come back to them and talk like normal, invested human beings.

**Spoiler:** When I'm wrong, I'm REALLY wrong.

The night before, he had a complicated surgery, and I was just coming off a double shift. I went home to soak in my ginormous tub. The plan was to just meet up at my parent's house for lunch, and as per usual, I was running late.

**Pro Tip:** When you're walking in a car garage, pay attention.

I had my head down and was texting my mother that I would be a little late, but not to panic, and I was completely distracted by how exhausted I was. I was tired in bones that I didn't even know I had. I flipped my hair over my shoulder and suddenly, there it was.

It smelled sweet - the chloroform. I mean, I've seen it happen so many times in movies, and it's true, what happens, I mean.

It's true.

I passed out.
It felt like I was in and out for days.
And days.

In reality, it was more like twelve hours. And I only know that because in the months to come, I pieced everything together with news articles, conversations with Eli and my parents, and the meticulous notes that my boyfriend kept over the two days I was held hostage.

Because that's what I was now - a hostage.

I never showed up at my parent's house. Eli was there, and he checked the clock above my mother's head so many times that she finally got up to check on me. She went to the kitchen to get out her phone, but I didn't answer her call. And I didn't answer her follow-up text.

Eli started to pace.

**Sidenote:** I know what you're thinking. I know because I've heard it at least a thousand times since. What was a billionaire lottery winner doing without a bodyguard? Why wasn't she more aware?

Such good questions, and I just don't know the answers to them. Hindsight is 20/20, and you better believe *that* situation has been rectified.

No one - not one time did *anyone* ever suspect something like this would happen. I took self-defense in college, but I never imagined that I'd be in this ... position. It was a monumental oversight.

My dad eventually went to the garage. Meticulously, he cleaned shelves. Swept. Later, he would tell me that all he could think about was that day I had come to him to tell him about Sadie.

Eli was the first to suggest they call Sean after three hours had passed with no word from me. My mom and dad agreed. Not one part of me even wants to think about how hard all of this must have been on them.

Sean called the police.

Sitting in my parent's living room, a detective asked a billion questions. Eli's handwriting tried to keep track of most of them on a notepad from the kitchen, but it was all mostly chicken scratch that he acquired in med school.

Turns out, when you're talking about Cincinnati's "darling lottery winner", things move pretty quickly. *Easily*, they figured out it was Lawson. Security footage was *easily* obtained. His face was *easily* recognized.

Not Easy: Watching me unsuspectingly walk to my car texting my mom.
Not Easy: Watching me struggle against him.
Not Easy: Watching me fall limply to the ground.
Not Easy: Watching Lawson drag me to my car.

He was gone.
I was gone.
Vanished.
Hostage.

## Lesson #10

**Reckoning: A settling of accounts**

**The Travertys were about to have a reckoning.**

I was out there, though.

My memories are sketchy. My dreams were wild. I was always running. I'd wake up in a haze, look around only long enough to see Lawson staring at me.

A green couch.
Cigarette smoke.
A TV turned up too loud.
A blanket that smelled sweet.
Food containers.

And then, he'd give me something, and I'd be out again.

How long was it? I don't know. I have no grasp. No way of knowing.

I couldn't even lift my thousand-pound head off of the couch. Minutes were just ... years.

...

Eli didn't sleep. In his notes, his handwriting blurs. Lists of possible accomplices. A note of what I was wearing. Names of patients I helped that had died. Words trail off as he dozed. One word was written over a dozen times or so, and it was *Sarah*. He made the connection before anyone else, and he told the police about the letters.

Detectives analyzed phone records, talked to neighbors, looked at security footage from around my apartment, but aside from being able to tell that Lawson took a left out of the parking garage, they had nothing else.

When Lawson woke me up finally, I was tied to the couch. I had been for a while based on how swollen, sore, raw, and bloody my wrists were. He stared at me. Was he high? I couldn't tell.

"Lawson?" I asked weakly. I struggled against the rope. "Untie me? Please?"

"You deserve all of this, you know." He sneered at me. He wasn't high. He was *angry*. So incredibly angry.

"Because of the press?" I tried to reason. "We can send out a retraction." I paused to cough up my right lung. What the hell had he given me? I felt so ... broken, or something. I couldn't make myself think. "Is this about money? Do you need money?" I struggled to breathe, to sit up, to think.

"This isn't about your damn money, Grace. Everything isn't always about you." Suddenly, he stood and kicked a nearby trash can. I jumped against my bonds and it shot pain up my arms. My eyes widened when he suddenly started laughing. "This is about *Sadie*." His eyes cut into me and he leaned in so close I could smell the McDonald's he'd eaten for lunch. My stomach rolled. "This is about what you fucking did to Sadie Traverty."

My throat ran dry, my whole entire body stilled, and I looked at him in the eye. "What the hell are you talking about?" I was missing something, but I couldn't quite piece it together.

"That's right, you bitch. *Sadie*." He slapped me - just because he could ... I think. And damn, it burned.

I stared at him. I almost didn't want to know. I didn't want to know how she found him, and sunk her teeth into him. I didn't want to know how she wrapped around him like some kind of poisonous snake. I didn't want to know the lies she told him, or how she instigated this whole mess. I didn't want to know. I just wanted to go home.

"Lawson," I whispered. "What has she done to you?"

"Not a damn thing that I didn't want her to, Grace." He stood up and walked to the counter. Trees were out the kitchen window. Where were we? A cabin? It all felt small.

Remote.
Shit.

"How did she find you?" I watched him fill a coffee cup like he didn't have a hostage on his couch. Like he was a carefree man that wasn't committing about a dozen different felonies.

"After that stupid news article, I started getting letters from her. And then, I started visiting." He turned and stalked towards me. I flinched. "She has a very interesting story to tell, Gracie-Baby."

At that, I did heave. I turned as much as I could and threw up bile from my stomach. Gracie-Baby. The sound of that stupid nickname and the way he whispered it so ... *lovingly* ... made me want to throw up for the rest of my life.

"What do you even mean?" I shivered suddenly. It was cold. Was there not any heat in this freaking place? Where *was* I?

He sat next to me on the couch and stroked my cheek. I immediately pulled away as far as I could. "Sadie's baby. The baby you killed, remember? Or has all of that money suddenly given you amnesia?" He slapped me again and I could taste the blood on my lip.

He was out of his damn mind. "That's not what happened," my voice cracked. I was so tired, and I didn't understand any of this. "That's not what happened at all."

"Even now? Here?" He gestured around this ... was it a cabin? "You can't even fucking admit it *here*? Just *say it*, Grace. Let the truth set you FREE!" He yelled too dramatically, and then he laughed too hard.

Remote.
A rock landed in my stomach and I knew then.

I wasn't going to live through this.

"You killed someone else's baby, and then you let your best friend take the fall for it. Isn't that right?" In his fury, this time - he punched me hard over and over again in the side of the ribs. I couldn't breathe. I couldn't think. I saw stars. I saw so many stars. I heard a crack. I felt something give way.

"No," I whispered back, in raging pain. "I didn't even know she was pregnant!"

He vigorously shook his head. "Such bullshit. Such *utter* bullshit." He paced over to the door and I tensed - half expecting an escaped Sadie to waltz right on in. Instead, he turned his head over to me and was suddenly completely calm. "Soon," he whispered. "*Soon*."

...

With the letters from "Sarah" and the incoming calls from the prison, they had it figured out. Sadie was the mastermind. Detectives were dispatched to pay her a visit, and a different set were sent to the home of the Travertys.

All of these years later, and they still hadn't moved. That same creek was still at the back of their house. The woods were still lining the creek bed. Their home remained unchanged.

When my parents pulled up with the police, I wonder if they, too, felt the crippling onslaught of dejavu. Again, my dad greeted them at the door. This time, Eli was there and not me.

Eli's notes are so precise:

*Grace had on an apron with rabbits. She met me, Morgan, and Caroline with concerned eyes. How long had it been since they'd seen each other? Shook their hands. Wondered how they'd produced a murderer, or a mastermind. Grace T. invited us in and offered cookies. Detectives French and Johnson obliged and I stared at them. How could they eat?*

*Questions all over the place -*

*When had they seen Sadie last?*
*- Mom: 2 Weeks ago*
*- Dad: Not since sentencing (odd?)*
*- Mom: Cried*
*- Dad: Stoic*

*Did she mention Grace?*
*- Mom: At every visit. Always asks.*
*- Mom always fills her in.*
*Grace T. looked at me - "I told her about you"*
*Grace T. glanced at Caro - "I read about him in the papers."*

*SHIT.*

*Did she seem erratic? Anxious?*
*- Mom: Always*

*SHIT SHIT.*

*Did she mention a "Sarah" to you?*
*- Mom: I mean ... that's her real name? We've called her Sadie as a nickname ... her whole life.*
*- Dad: You call her that. I don't call her a damn thing.*
*- Dad: Hardened*

*Her name is SARAH?*
** Mental Note: When she gets back, ask Grace if she knew.*

[For the record, I didn't have a damn clue. I was best friends with that girl for sixteen years and as it turns out, there's a lot of things I didn't know.]

From Eli's notes, the questions lasted four hours. The sun was setting on Day 2. My mom needed meds to sleep. Dr. Hall prescribed them.

Was I asleep? I didn't know. I know I was dreaming, but how had I fallen asleep? I was in Sadie's bathroom, covered in blood. I wanted to scream, but nothing came out.

Instead, a bruising palm crashed across my cheek. "It's time." Lawson was putting on a jacket. Out the window, I could see that it was dark outside. He untied me and I immediately fought him. No way was I going out there. No way was I going anywhere with him. In the end, he had to zip tie my hands, and duct tape my mouth. Tears trailed down my face. I fought the panicked feeling of not being able to breath, not being able to move.

Was this it? Was this the end?
He yanked my ponytail.
That's when I heard his gun.

He had a GUN? How the hell did he get a GUN? I was shrieking behind the tape and panicking and stalling and pushing my butt up against him and NO. I didn't not want to walk through that door to whatever it was that was out there. I would not go easily. No way in hell.

The barrel of the gun dug into my back and into what I was sure was a broken rib. Even the blinding pain wasn't enough for me to settle the F back down. "Walk. You try to run and I'll shoot you in the back." He stabbed at my kidney. "GO."

My feet felt like cinder blocks, but in the end - I walked forward. He shoved me into the trunk of the dang car, and he roped together my kicking feet. He looked down at me and I shook my head at him. He only shrugged. With the loudest thud I've ever heard, the trunk lid shut.

How far away from home was I?

[Answer: About thirty minutes. I was at the Miami Whitewater Forest. Freaking Lawson. He had me all holed up like the Unabomber.]

It felt like we drove forever. I tried to take deep breaths, but it was impossible because I was so terrified. My rib was definitely broken. Maybe two? I tried to steady myself – to catalog my wounds, but not knowing when turns were coming made it impossible. Every jostle felt like a knife stabbing me in the chest.

Blessedly, I finally felt us slow down. Were we back in Cincinnati?

...

*Finally, Caroline slept.*
*Detectives back from prison.*
*Saw Sadie.*
*She had a lawyer.*
*Travertys funding that lawyer? Double check tomorrow.*
*Said she'd only smile at them.*
*What kind of person?*

*When was the last time I told Grace I loved her? When was the last time I pulled her to me in bed? What did she smell like? God. I miss her.*

...

The trunk popped open and a gun was aimed right at my chin. I didn't move. I didn't even breathe.

Lawson sneered.

He jerked me up by my shirt and with the biggest knife, sliced the rope off of my feet. "Walk," he ordered again.

I got out of the trunk and looked around. I recognized where I was almost immediately.

Shit.

In the distance, I could see the Traverty home, and the neighborhood looked mostly the same. There were a few new houses. I hadn't been over here in ten years. It was all so different, but all so much the same. Lawson shoved me. I screamed from the pain into my duct tape. I started walking.

We trudged through the grass, past a home with no lights on, and down to the damn creek. It still smelled the same - like disgusting wet, moldy dirt. From what I could tell, it was the middle of the night. The stars shined so brightly. I'll never forget that. I will just … I will just never forget that.

We were now out of view of the Traverty home, and way out of hearing range from the other homes. That's when he ripped the duct tape from my mouth. I screamed, and then he slapped me again. Would this ever end?

There was no way for me to run, and really - I wouldn't have gotten far. He would've shot me, I'm sure of it. He stopped me in the middle of the soft creek bed, and I felt my feet sink into the sand. I closed my eyes. I took a deep breath. I waited for the reckoning.

## Lesson #11

**Absolution: Formal release from guilt, obligation, or punishment.**

**And maybe God would absolve her, but I never would.**

There was food in his teeth. How I saw that in the dark of night, I'll never understand, but there it was. He was so angry that spittle flew out of his mouth and onto my cheek, and his gun dragged down my arm. "The time has come, Gracie Morgan. *Your* time."

He shoved me forward and I stumbled. Was this the time? Was this the time I needed to start begging for my life? I looked around the sand and hoped for some kind of stick, or a rock. Anything I could use to defend myself. "Lawson," I cried out. "Stop!"

He trained his gun on me, and he pulled something from his dirty hoodie pocket. It was a folded-up piece of paper. What the fuck? He smiled at me and for as long as I live, I will never forget that smile.

"Sadie sent something for you. Call it a going away present." He laughed at his joke, but I stood as still as a statue and wept.

"Dear Grace Morgan," he started in some sort of theatrical way.

I was going to die on this creek bed.

At that same moment, in the house behind me, Lawrence Traverty awoke and realized that his wife was nowhere to be found. Fearing the worst, he phoned the detective that had left his card earlier that day. His voice quickened as he checked every room in the house. Lights blazed in the dark, and Grace was gone. In the living room, he looked out over the deck, and into the darkness. He knew the creek was out there. He shivered.

I had no idea, but the Calvary was coming. I had no idea, but help was on the way. I just had no idea what was about to happen.

On his way over to the Traverty house, Detective French called Eli and my parents.

...

*The detective called.*
*G. Trav. is missing.*
*Headed there now.*
*Will wait with Lawrence.*
*Is GT involved? Did they take her, too?*
*I'm going to have to pay to replace the carpet at the Morgans. I've paced so much that there's a track now.*

*Grace? We're coming, baby.*

...

Lawson continued to read in the most dramatic fashion I've ever heard. "And it was because of you and your perfect little fucking life that I had to kill my baby." That part must've shocked the hell out of him because he stopped there to reread the line. He stared at the paper.

I stepped backwards once. Twice. By the time he looked up, I was almost up the creek bed. He lunged for me and dragged me back down. And then he beat the shit out of me. Punches and kicks and I was writhing on the ground desperately trying to stop the blows.

"That's enough," her cool voice commanded.

Grace. Fucking. Traverty. I'd recognize that voice out of a sea of thousands.

"Who's there?" Lawson whipped his gun around and pointed into the darkness.

She stepped out closer to us, and there she was. The moon illuminated her pale, stricken face. I pulled myself off the ground in a haze. I was covered in wet sand. Was she part of this, too? My brain just wouldn't … couldn't work.

"I'm Sadie's mother." Her eyes darted to me and I saw her shock. Relief washed over me. Maybe she wasn't a part of this shit show. Maybe she was going to save me. Timidly, I stepped towards her. "She told me to come down here at midnight. She told me you'd have something for me. What did the rest of the letter fucking SAY, Lawson?!" she shrieked into the darkness.

She didn't move to help me.
She *didn't move* to *help* me.

Lawson didn't budge, either. "What do you mean? Sadie told you to come?"

Grace was unmoved. "Read the damn letter, Lawson." She screamed again.

And then she pulled out a small pistol. It was shiny and fit perfectly in her delicate hands. What was with these freaking people all suddenly having guns? I edged away from them both. There was about to be a shootout, and I could sense it. And believe me when I tell you - I wanted NO part in it.

Shocked, Lawson slowly picked up the paper from the ground. His hand shook. I pushed back up the sand even more. Every inch hurt, but every inch was one step closer to not being on the creek bed anymore.

"And I found out I was pregnant," Lawson read. His voice quivered. "You were too stupid, Grace. You couldn't figure it out. We were barely sixteen. I hadn't slept with any *boy*. You know that, Grace."

I watched Sadie's mom. Was she writing to me? Was she writing to her? I couldn't tell. What the fuck was happening?

Lawson's voice cracked, but he continued reading the letter. "Except my," and here … he paused. And I don't think it was to be dramatic. I think it was because what he was about to say? What he was about to say was a certain kind of bad that even Lawson – a hostage taking criminal couldn't imagine.

"Except my dad." He continued. "No one would've believed that he was the father. But I thought maybe you might. You never wanted to listen. You never fucking wanted to listen." He glanced up at Grace, his eyes wide. He obviously hadn't read the letter before he came tonight, and he was just as shocked as I was.

I searched my brain. That day she was so cavalier. She hadn't wanted to tell me anything else. I was sure of it. I chewed my lip. We were babies ourselves, and I was positive that I remembered everything from that day. That's when I heard Grace gasp beside me.

Lawson continued. "If my mother is there," he stopped, and cleared his throat. Quietly, he read on.

"WHAT THE FUCK DOES IT SAY," she screamed. In my head, I screamed right along with her. Why wasn't I running? Why was I staying to listen and watch this pan out? Even now, I couldn't tell you. My feet were frozen to the cold ground.

"If my mother is there," he started again. "If she actually showed up for me for once, you tell her this is all her fault for looking the other way for so long." His voice trailed off.

In slow motion, Lawson's eyes raised up off of the paper in front of him.

His eyes met Grace Traverty's.

His eyes widened when she raised her arm.

His arms went up in the air, and the letter was dropped.

And when Grace pulled the trigger, his eyes went blank.

I turned and ran. I ran so hard and so fast that I almost didn't stop when I hit the Traverty lawn. Another shot rang out and I was certain it was her firing at me. She missed. I kept running. I hit their side yard and tripped over a sprinkler head. I got up, and I kept running.

When I hit the front yard, Detective French was pulling into the driveway. It was a miracle. One of so many during those dark days.

His sirens came on when he saw me, and as he parked in the driveway, I collapsed next to his car door. He yelled my name in relief, as I motioned towards the creek. His partner came around to the front of the car with his gun drawn. He ran off with his flashlight to the creek bed.

I gasped for air, and clawed at French's uniform. "She shot him! She shot him and she's down there, and I watched her shoot him! She fucking pulled the trigger!" My words flowed out of my mouth and nothing would calm me down.

French cut off my zip ties and I had forgotten they were even there. How did I even get up the hill with my hands zip tied? "Grace. Shhhhh. Slow down. Are you okay? God, I'm so glad to see you. We've been looking everywhere. Shhhhhh." He used his radio to call for an ambulance and backup.

Lawrence Traverty came outside just then, and with a hidden fury that had been building for years, I ran at him. Scratching and clawing and screaming at him. "You bastard," I shouted at him. "You fucking did this to them. YOU DID THIS TO THEM." I punched and kicked him, and he didn't even fight back.

French pulled me off of him, and then asked him to sit in the back of the police car. "Grace," French's soothing voice was some kind of balm to my confused and broken body, and this time, when I collapsed, I didn't get back up. He sat me on the steps of the porch, and sirens wailed in the distance. "The ambulance is coming, Grace. Just hold on."

As we waited for the inevitable, he looked me over. "Are you okay?" Gently, he touched my eye. It was swelling shut, and I'm sure I was bleeding from more places than one. "We've been looking everywhere for you," he whispered, shaking his head in obvious relief.

I was sobbing uncontrollably. "It was him," I kept saying. "It was him. Sadie said he was the father of her own baby. Her dad did this to her." I pointed shakily at the car and in the streetlights, I could see Lawrence's head bowed. My tears flowed unabated. "He did this to his own daughter." I gagged, and what was even in my stomach to throw up?

French looked over his shoulder at his police car just as his partner came up the hill. "Are they alive?" I shouted. I tried to stand. French tried to hold me back. "Are they alive?" I asked again and again. They exchanged some sort of silent communication and I saw their faces fall.

"Oh my God," I screamed. I think I was maybe going to scream for the rest of my life. I couldn't calm down. "Oh my God, she killed him!"

And then there were police cars. Police car after police car. Ambulances. Neighbors out on their front lawns. So many people were running everywhere. I was dizzy and exhausted and in so much pain. I think my heart was broken.

As an EMT shined his penlight into my eyes, and as he asked me what day it was, there was Eli. Pushing through the throng, there he was and my parents were right behind him. I think time stood still. His brown winter coat flapped in the middle of the night wind. The red of the police lights flashed over his stubble, and the minute his eyes hit mine - I knew. I was his. Forever. Not a chance in hell that I belong to anyone else.

Mercy.
Miracles.

I clung to my family and vowed to never let them go ever again. I sobbed into Eli's jacket - my blood marring his lapel. I held my mom's hand so tightly, I thought it would break. My dad smoothed his hand over my tangled, sandy hair. "She killed him," I wailed over and over. "She just killed him. I watched her just kill him."

And that's when my legs finally gave out.

It had been almost three days of constant terror.
It was two gunshots.
It was countless kicks and punches.
Slaps.

Duct tape.
Zip ties.

It all just felt like cement bricks on my shoulders, and I just *collapsed*. They rushed me back into the ambulance. As they checked me over, I watched two gurneys go past out the small windows - each of them in a body bag.

And that's when I realized Lawson wasn't the only victim of the creek bed that night.
And that's when I realized Grace Traverty had committed suicide.
And that's when I think I must have passed out.

I woke up in the same hospital I walked into every single day for work. My mom and dad were asleep. Eli sat vigil next to me. His eyes were tired, and his hand grasped mine. Was I dreaming? Was it really all over?

I cleared my thick, hurting throat. "What happened?" I whispered. My eyelids felt like lead.

Eli blinked back at me. Tears shined in his eyes. He glanced up at the monitors, and then back down to me. "You passed out last night."

I squeezed his hand and relief washed over me in waves. "I thought …" Tears filled my own eyes. "I thought I'd never … Oh my God, I thought ..."

He squeezed my hand back. "Shhhhh," he whispered through tears. "I would've found you." He leaned in and kissed my bruised forehead. "I would've found you if it was the last thing I ever did." His voice was rough, and he nuzzled my neck. "I would've never stopped looking, Grace."

Like bricks falling from the sky, it came back to me in blows. "She killed him, Eli," I said for the thousandth time. "I watched her pull the trigger, and I watched Lawson drop to the ground." He nodded his head and it occurred to me that he probably knew more than I did at this point. "How long have I been out? What happened?"

I looked over to my parents stirring on their makeshift bed. "Mom? Dad? What happened?" The three of them shared a glance. Quietly, mom and dad got up and walked over to my bed. My mom's warm fingers brushed through my matted hair. My dad wound his fingers through mine.

Eli took a deep breath. "Grace is dead, too. Detective French found the letter, and he put it all together." He searched my face. "Lawrence confessed to being the father of Sadie's child." Eli dropped his head to my hand.

"He's been arrested," my dad continued. "He'll be gone for a long time."

"And Sadie?" I asked. "Sadie was just a kid, mom. Sadie was a kid and her dad — her dad was doing all of that to her and no one was there to help her."

My mom nodded her head sadly. "I know, baby. Now, maybe she'll have some peace. And maybe she'll get the help she needs."

In prison.

She left off the "in prison" part because we all knew that Sadie Traverty was never getting back out. Not after all of this, anyway.

I closed my eyes, exhausted to my very core. We would talk about these three days a thousand more times in the coming months, I was sure. But for right now? For right this second? Nothing mattered more to me than sleeping right here, surrounded by people that would fight for me.

And *always* find me.

## Lesson #12

**Faith: Complete trust or confidence in someone or something.**

**I had faith in myself, and I had faith in the future.**

Being a patient is hard when your sole purpose is to care for patients. I was frustrated, impatient, ready to be free of IVs, and constant observation. Elijah left my care up to the fantastic Dr. Hall, but he was there every single step of the way. It was a blessing to have a boyfriend that also happened to be one of the best doctors in his field, but I'm pretty sure he was about to give himself an ulcer based on the worrying over me he was doing.

I escaped the three day hostage situation with only two broken ribs and a concussion. It was another miracle - especially with the beatings I took. Before I was discharged, Dr. Hall came in to visit one last time. He was a nice man with a friendly face. His eyes gave him away every single time, though. And after working with him so many different times, I knew something was up.

"Eli. Good to see you again." He shook Eli's hand, and walked over to my bed. He looked me over, before calling over his shoulder. "Why don't you guys give us some privacy, okay?"

Automatically, my parents stood to leave. Eli stood like a pilar - unmoving.

"Over my dead body, Hall. I just got her back; I'm not leaving her side." He crossed his arms in protest.

"Dr. Heatherton. I'll not ask again. I'd like to speak to my patient in confidence." He raised his greying eyes at my pit bull of a boyfriend.

I looked from one doctor to the other. Something was serious going on. I've seen that face on Dr. Hall in the operating room - generally right before things go pear-shaped. "Eli? Give us a couple of minutes?" I took a deep breath, fortifying myself for ... I didn't know what.

After a few more protests, he finally relented. Compromising, he stood right outside my closed door. When it finally latched behind him, Dr. Hall took my hand.

"What's going on?" I asked. My voice shook and my hand clenched on its own accord.

"You know Eli, right? He's been obsessed with you ever since you came in. He reviews your charts and chides the nurses. He's been hellfire for the past few days." He smiled down at me.

I'm pretty sure that violated about a thousand different rules, but I stayed quiet. I wasn't going to complain, and I'm pretty sure that wasn't Hall's point.

He cleared his throat. "There was something that I didn't put in your chart, Grace. Something you need to know about before you go home." He rubbed the back of my hand with his thumb.

"What is it? An allergy? A brain bleed? Am I dying? What's the deal?" I smiled and searched his face for an answer. I found nothing.

"You're pregnant, Grace." He smiled at me. "It's still very early. Six weeks, or so. I wanted you to know that you need to see someone when you hit that twelve week mark, okay? And when you come in for your follow up care, make sure that they note it in your chart. I just ..." He paused and looked back at the door. "I just wanted you to know first. I don't know. I just felt like it was the right thing to do."

I blinked back at him. Pregnant? That just wasn't *fucking* possible. Was it? When was my last period? I couldn't remember. There was too much haze and discord and *holy shit.*

I couldn't remember.

I swallowed ... and then swallowed again. I cleared my throat. "Are you sure?"

He nodded his head. "Yes, Grace. I'm sure. An ultrasound confirmed when we were looking for internal bleeding."

My chest felt heavy. I looked all around the room and felt it closing in. What a time for my anxiety to come roaring back to life. What a time for a panic attack. What a damn time to be alive. Through a tunnel, I heard Dr. Hall's voice.

"Grace? Breathe, Grace. Take deep breaths." He put the oxygen mask over my nose and mouth and in my head, I counted to ten over and over. "Breathe in," he coached. "Breathe out." He pressed my call button, and a nurse that I love came in.

Elijah came in right behind her. “What the fuck happened, Hall?” He unbuttoned his cuffs and rolled up his sleeves. He lowered my bed, and suddenly, my room lights were right in my eyes. I gasped in my mask.

I heard Dr. Hall murmur something to the nurse, and then I felt it. The warm sensation of medicine designed to calm me down floating through my IV. My breathing slowed. My muscles relaxed.

“Grace? Look over at me, okay?” My eyes drifted over to Dr. Hall, and his concern washed over me. “Better?”

I nodded my head. “I’m good,” I whispered through my mask.

“Somebody needs to tell me what the fuck just happened,” Eli roared over me. He was tired. On edge. Who knows when he had last slept. Normally, he was so even-tempered, but I think this was it. This was the straw that broke him.

Dr. Hall looked at me and I nodded my head. “Grace is pregnant, Eli.”

And the blood rushed from his face.
And his jaw dropped to the floor.
And his hand fell away from mine.
And he took a step back from my bed.
And then another.
And then he was out the door.
And then he was gone.

Here’s the thing. The Cincinnati Billionaire was also now The Cincinnati Billionaire Who Was Kidnapped, Beaten, and Tossed Into The Center of The Traverty Saga. The press was bad before, but now they were relentless.

Poor Megan Rhodes (PR Woman of the Year) was really earning her keep around me. To the press, she released a stunning black and white photo of me and Elijah together in the hospital. I was hugging his neck, and my face wasn’t visible. What was visible - even in the black and white - were the ugly marks on my wrist, and the bruises on my arms.

She released a carefully crafted statement that assured the public I was fine, but also, she left zero room for interpretation. I was simply unavailable. There would be no interviews. There would be no more photos. There would be no more statements after this. There would just be ... no more.

It took a team to get me from my hospital room down to the basement garage. A limousine pulled up, and I was settled in the back - far away from the prying eyes of the public. It wasn't like I could really see them anyway. Between the darkened windows on that car and my swollen eyes, I was lucky I could even tell what color shirt I had on. My mom sat on my left. My dad sat on my right. I took deep, deep breaths. In through my nose and out through my mouth, and -

Elijah was still gone.

Blessedly, my parents didn't even ask.

Home felt surreal. It was like I had changed. Everything had changed. But my apartment was exactly the same. The bread was still on the counter. My pumpkin spice candle was on the bar. My bed was still unmade. I took a deep breath, and cried.

And the tears wouldn't stop.

And then I got so angry.

Because I was so tired of crying. I was so tired of feeling weak. I was tired of every single part of my body hurting. I was tired of how much work it took to take a deep breath. I was so tired of not feeling in control. I was so tired of feeling like people needed to treat me like glass.

I shoved the candle off of the bar and it shattered on the tile floor. I shoved the place settings off of the breakfast table and was satisfied to hear them crash to the floor, too. It felt good to throw the vase and watch the flowers fly. And it felt good to knock down every damn barstool in my kitchen.

I turned and looked at the shocked faces of my parents. "I need to shower," I said, looking over my shoulder at the mess I made. "Leave it." I knew that before I even hit the carpet of my bedroom, my dad would be on his hands and knees cleaning up the glass.

"Grace," she called out to me, as I walked away. "Let me help you." She trailed behind me knowing I'd have a terrible time getting my shirt off over my head, or lathering the shampoo, or washing my face. Every movement hurt, every breath hurt, and if Lawson wasn't already dead, I'd probably kill him with my own two hands.

As soon as my ribs were healed, anyway.

Nothing is as humbling as having your mom help you shower. Or use the bathroom. She was so gentle and so loving, that I sobbed into her shoulder. I was a grown woman, and I needed her now more than ever.

A baby.
A baby.
A baby.

I was now a mother to a baby.

She brushed my wet hair and I looked at her face in the mirror. She looked as tired as I felt. There were lines around her face that hadn't been there a week ago, and her hair was greying. "I'm pregnant," I whispered.

The brush stilled in my long hair, and her hand fell on my shoulder. "Grace? Are you serious?" Her mouth dropped in wonder. A small breath puffed out from her lungs.

A movie flickered in my head. Kidnapped. Beaten. Bruised. The letter. Sadie. Grace. Lawson. Ambulances. Recovery. The shattered glass in the kitchen. A baby. Repeat. Kidnapped. Beaten. Bruised. The letter. Sadie. Grace. Lawson. Ambulances. Recovery. The shattered glass in the kitchen. A baby. Rewind. Kidnapped. Beaten. Bruised. The letter. Sadie. Grace. Lawson. Ambulances. Recovery. The shattered glass in the kitchen. A baby.

A baby.
A baby.
A baby.

I was going to be a mom.

I nodded my head and smiled for what felt like the first time in years. "I am. Dr. Hall thought I was maybe six or seven weeks along."

She dropped down and gave me the biggest hug, and I didn't even feel the pang of hurt in my ribs. "I'm going to be a grandma," she shrieked, and that must've got my dad's attention. He came barreling into my bathroom.

"Grace? Caroline? What's going on?" He took in my mother's utter jubilation, and my tear-soaked face and I can see why he would've been confused. I wonder if I will ever stop scaring the holy shit out of them.

"Grace is pregnant! Can you believe that?!" She hugged my shoulders tight again and I winced, but this bubbling up of excitement and love and anticipation felt better than anything else had in what felt like years.

"You're kidding!" My dad's face broke out into its own goofy grin, and he stood tall, bouncing on his feet. "That's wonderful, kid!"

"A fall baby? Is that what it will be? Oh, this is so exciting!" My mom picked the brush back off of the floor. "My baby is having her own baby," she mused.

"Are ya hungry? How about I go order us a celebration dinner?" Laughing, my dad shook his head and left the bathroom. "Praise the Lord," I heard him say, as he turned the corner.

Praise the Lord, indeed. For good news, finally ... For good news.

Her brush got stuck on a tangle and my head jerked in response. "Oh, sorry, honey." She worked on it in silence for a second or two, and then the question came that I knew she'd been holding in for a long time.

"What's Eli have to think about all of this?"

"I don't know, mom." And that was the loudest, biggest truth I'd said in days. "I just don't know." My jaw trembled. I feel like I'd been crying now for six years.

There's a funny thing about moms that we can all acknowledge. They know things. They know things like when to be quiet, and when to push. They know how to ask specific questions, and they know how to help us get to the answers.

"Why don't you ask him?" The tangle finally broke, and she resumed brushing my hair. Her question clanked around in my head. *Why don't you ask him?*

That night, we had a celebration dinner of spaghetti and green beans and garlic bread and the best sparkling grape juice this side of everything. I helped my mom sweep up my mess, but I still couldn't bring myself to be sorry about it.

We watched Netflix until my eyes were heavy, until my dad was snoozing in the recliner, and until my mom was snoring next to me. When I stood up to go to bed, they got up, too. My mom tucked me into bed, and my mom flipped on the light in my closet.

"Do you want me to sleep with you tonight?" She sat on the edge of the bed and brushed her hand through my hair.

I looked around, and then back to her. The circles under her eyes were dark and I knew how tired she probably was. "No. I think I'll be okay."

"If you need anything," my dad whispered as he hugged me, "just call out. We'll come. We'll always come."

And there have never been words that rang more true.

I spent the first night in my bed and it felt too big. The covers were soft and the pillows were cool, but Elijah wasn't there. In the morning, I resolved to text him or call him. To ask him where he's been. To ask him why he always fucking seems to leave without a word.

It felt like my eyes had only been closed for a second before my cell phone went off on my nightstand. Without even checking to see who was calling, I answered. "Yes?"

"Ms. Morgan? I have Dr. Heatherton here. He'd like to see you."

Marco. He was part of the new security force that Marshall and Sean put together for me. It was Marco's alert voice that greeted me on the phone. He was standing outside my apartment door, and it felt good to know that someone was always there watching me.

"Ms. Morgan?" he prompted.

I wiped my eyes. "Yes. Sorry. Send him in." I slowly rolled over and flipped my nightstand light on, grimacing at how bright it was, and how much it hurt to shift. Slowly, I sat up, and slowly, I wrapped my robe around my shoulders. My chest ached, and my body felt so heavy. It felt like I was going to be this tired for the rest of my life. I heard the door open and shut, and I waited. No way was I going to him.

"Grace?" His gruff voice called to me from the doorway. "Can I come in?"

I shrugged my shoulders. "Looks like we're past that point already, don't you think?"

He stepped into my bedroom and toed off his shoes. "Can we talk?" I nodded my head and gestured to the foot of my bed. He looked exhausted. He looked like I felt.

"Where have you been, Elijah?" There. Just like my mom told me to do. I asked him. My mouth went dry as I waited for him to form an answer.

He sighed and dropped his head into his hands. "I went back to Georgia. I went back to Georgia and saw Sarah and her parents. I told him." He sighed heavily again and stood up. "It just all felt like too much, you know? I almost lost you, Grace. I *almost lost you.* And I already lost Sarah. And I already lost a baby. And here we were again? It almost happened to me a-fucking-gain?"

He stood and paced the floor, and I sat and watched. I was so happy to see him, but still so pissed that he left me. "Yea. But it didn't."

He didn't even hear me. "So I went back home and I asked her parents *why*. I asked why it had to be like this at all. Her mom gave me some kind of bullshit answer about the hurts leaving holes in our hearts for more love to come in and I almost threw up." He ran his hand through his hair for the thousandth time. "And they're better. Her parents, I mean. They're better than I've ever seen them look. I almost *lost* you, Grace. I almost lost you and I would've never, ever recovered." He looked over at me and it almost gutted me. "But when I think about almost losing you AND our baby?" He shook his head and tears filled his eyes. Some kind of sorrowful sound from the depths of him rose up and out. I was certain I NEVER wanted to hear that sound ever, ever again.

But all I could focus on was *our* baby. He said *our baby*, and it rushed around my head. I slowly scooted over so that he could join me in bed. "You left me," I whispered, my tears matching his.

Our baby.
Our baby.
*Our* baby.

AND OKAY. I know it isn't fair. I know he basically tore down mountains for me and didn't sleep for days and searched and searched and searched and then sat by my hospital bed and took care of me and yes. I KNOW. I know maybe I was acting a little "woe is me", but there is no guidebook here for how to act after being kidnapped.

"I did," he acknowledged. "I did." He climbed in next to me, and gently, he wrapped his arm around me. "I hadn't slept well for days. I was a mess. And you were having a panic attack and then, hey! You're pregnant. I just couldn't process anything. I just ... couldn't process it."

He dropped a kiss onto my forehead and even though it hurt, I cuddled in closer to him. He smelled like an airport and his cologne. "I stopped by my house and I hadn't been there since before … and it felt like too much there, too." Another kiss. "And so I went to the only people I knew would understand." Another kiss. "I'm so sorry, Grace."

I nodded my head as tears leaked out of my eyes. "Don't do it again, okay?"

I felt him nod his head next to me. “I love you more than I ever thought possible.” His voice was gruff in my ear. He pulled the blanket over us, and cuddled down next to me.

“I love you, too,” I whispered. “I love you so much, too.”

He turned and shut off the nightstand light. “Can I stay the night? I’m so tired.”

And you know what? I think that man was out before I even said yes.

## Lesson #13

**Truth: That which is true or in accordance with fact or reality.**

**The truth will set you free.**

The healing came slowly. I attended therapy sessions with my parents, by myself, and with Elijah. All of us went. All of us worked towards healing. The bruises faded. My ribs healed. I quit my job at the hospital. And I threw myself full time into Sarah's Faith - the foundation that Eli and I created together.

Elijah sold his house and moved in with me. We bumped into each other in the evenings in the best kind of way. Seeing his forks mixed in with mine filled me with hope. His coffee cups next to the coffee machine made me so happy. And sleeping with him each night gave me the feeling of safety that I craved.

The sentencing date for Lawrence loomed over our shoulders. This just felt like the last hurdle we would face before we could put the whole Traverty Travesty behind us. Between now and then, Megan prepped me on how to handle the press, my therapist prepped me on how to handle seeing Lawrence and possibly Sadie. Eli prepped me on how he'd never leave my side, and my parents just ... worried.

When the date finally arrived, I put on black dress and a long black coat that somehow hid my growing bump. On the lapel, I pinned a pink ribbon for Faith. I pulled my hair back into a tight bun, marveling at how well my ribs had healed, and how my body was stretching to accommodate new life. I put on my sunglasses, and the big frames covered the pink scar that was left over below my eye. I picked up my bag, and met my family, Sean, and Megan in the great room of my apartment.

"Are we ready?" I asked, looking at the somber faces surrounding me. They nodded in return, and we headed for the door. A group of security guards were waiting for us, and I *still* marveled at that new normal. I was not about to live that kidnapped life again. No ma'am.

"I prepped for a brief press conference after the sentencing. These are your notes," Megan handed me a slip of paper. "Remember: eye contact, shoulders back, answer only the questions you want, and take zero shit." For some reason, it felt good to have her by my side.

"Thank you," I murmured. She nodded once in response.

"I'll be there the whole time," Elijah whispered. I squeezed his hand. My dad's hand fell on my shoulder and I would just have been lost without all of them.

We had come just ... so far. From the first time I timidly sat in front of a press conference after winning - what I thought would be - life changing money. Now, I felt like some kind of powerhouse. I was ready to take on the press and use them for good. I was ready to sit in a courtroom and watch a man I had looked up to for a large portion of my life get sentenced. I was ready to put this entire mess behind me, and it all felt so right. I felt like, for the first time in my life, an actual adult.

We were dragged into the courtroom by our security team, through an actual throng of people. There were protestors and press, bystanders, and family members. All were shouting, and all of them were pushing. "This isn't going to be the hardest part," Sean whispered. I only nodded.

Once inside the cold courtroom, I sat on a bench close enough to see the whites of Lawrence's eyes. I wanted to see every single reaction. I wanted to see every single time he blinked. And I wanted him to see me.

The bench was hard on my back, but next to me, Elijah was soft. My mom put her hand on mine and I knew - I wasn't alone. I glanced over to Lawrence and realized that he *was*.

In my months of therapy, I had come to a few conclusions. Sadie was a victim, too. And while she caused me *great* harm, she still deserved to have someone sit on that bench for her. She deserved to have someone fight for her eight-year-old self. Her ten-year-old self. Eleven. Twelve. Fifteen-year-old self. She deserved to have someone sit for her to hold her abuser accountable.

It was a cross I was willing to bear. Megan and I worked on my impact statement together. I practiced it with her standing in front of me. She critiqued my posture, she told me when to lift my eyes from the paper, and when to pause for effect. The last time I read the last sentence, she took a deep breath in. "For Faith," she said, and then she shuffled her things together, and left. I realized then, that I was not the only one that this was affecting.

Back in the courtroom, I watched Lawrence's attorney. His black hair was slicked back, and his double chin was ... pink. And puffy. His belly hung over his belt and I wondered what kind of man takes on a client like Lawrence Traverty. He tapped his pen on the large table, and chewed aggressively on his lower lip.

I had been terrified of a trial in the beginning. I didn't want to be put on the stand, and I didn't want the entire story to be dragged through the press again and again every single day. Thankfully, Lawrence did the first right thing he'd ever done in his whole damn life. He pleaded guilty.

When the prosecutors asked if I would deliver an impact statement for sentencing, I said yes without hesitation. Words started turning around in my head, and not one time did I regret my decision. I could do this - for Sadie. For Faith. For every single girl that never had anyone come to save them. For every single girl that didn't get a chance to be a kid. For every single girl that suffered at the hands of her dad - quietly.

In unbearable silence.

I would do it for them.

"All rise," a bailiff called. As one, my entire row rose. Feet shuffled behind me. The judge walked in. His kind eyes were hidden behind bifocals, and his black robes swished as he walked up the steps to his seat.

Sean walked me through what would happen, and I was so thankful that I had time to prepare for the moment that the judge asked if Lawrence had anything to say for himself.

The man, the same age as my own father, looked like he had aged decades in jail. His hands were handcuffed in front of him, his stubble was grey, and his hair was a wreck. It had grown out, and it looked as though he had quit brushing it completely. His orange uniform hung from his shoulders, and his eyes were clouded by new wrinkles.

He stood, and I took a quick breath in. "I do, Your Honor. I do have something to say." He cleared his throat, and his attorney shifted a single piece of paper in front of him. Slowly and awkwardly, he unfolded his glasses. He pushed them onto his face, and dropped his head to read from the typed words.

"I stand before you today as a broken man," he said. His voice sounded like sandpaper. "I have no excuses. I know I have hurt so many people." He paused and his body moved. His shoulders shifted somewhat in my direction, but it was as if he couldn't make himself fully look at me. Instead, he looked back at the judge. "I have hurt so many people. And in the wake of my poor decisions, I lost my wife, and I hurt my daughter. For that, I just ..." He cleared his throat and this - *this* was *not* enough. "I just want to say I'm sorry." The judge blinked back at him.

That was it. *That was it*, my brain screamed. That's all he could muster? Eli squeezed my hand and I shook my head. That was all he could say? Sorry 'bout that? A tear rolled down my mother's eye, and I could tell that she was still so devastated over the loss of an old friend.

Megan and Sean both shifted in their seats. I felt it. It was almost my turn. My stomach turned. I squeezed my eyes shut to help stave off the sudden onslaught of nausea.

I could do this.
I could do this.
I *could do this*.

I had to do this.

No one else was *left* to do this.

When it was finally my turn, time stopped. Clocks stood still. All I could hear was the breath in my chest as I sucked air in and out. It had been years - a journey with wild twists and turns and they all led me to this very second. Standing behind a podium with weathered wood where my hands would rest. Standing behind a podium in a packed courthouse of onlookers that were going to literally hang on my words. Standing behind a podium in front of the man that had molested one of my best friends. Standing behind a podium as a completely different person than I was all those years ago. Stronger. Convicted. Ready.

I adjusted the microphone. It was an act that Megan had taught me to buy more time. Truthfully, I needed a second to collect myself. But also? I wanted to see Lawrence squirm. I cleared my throat and he quickly glanced up at me. All I saw was ugly. A man with an ugly heart and a man with an ugly, scarred past. A man that had hurt the only people in his life that had truly mattered, and a man that carried a devastating secret in his front pocket for decades.

I licked my lips. I tasted the Chanel lipstick that I had so carefully applied in the car. The baby that I had found out about in the hospital right after my kidnapping kicked a leg, and isn't that how the timing of life goes? I wondered if Sadie had felt a baby kicking in her own belly all of those years ago.

I looked down at my paper, took in a deep breath, and began.

"My name is Grace Morgan, and I am here today to speak for the Sadie Traverty that was once my best friend. In the dark of one March night, Sadie - Lawrence's only daughter - delivered a healthy baby girl on the floor in her bathroom. She was alone. It was the baby that she had conceived after Lawrence had repeatedly raped her. She delivered a baby girl in her *bathroom*, and didn't know what to do. She didn't know what to do because -" I paused and looked at Lawrence - "how could she have known? After all, what was she supposed to do when her dad walked into her bedroom in the middle of the night and covered her mouth so she wouldn't scream? What was she supposed to do when her dad pulled her out of school in the middle of the day to satiate his sick needs? What was she supposed to do when he stumbled into her shower? And what was she supposed to do when he sat next to her on Sundays in the front pew of church?

"You were supposed to *protect* her, Lawrence. Instead, you *destroyed* her. You took giant chunks from her childhood and you helped her bury them in the backyard of your house. You took giant chunks from her childhood and you used them to wipe the blood off of her bathroom floor. You took giant chunks from her childhood and you used them to feel better about yourself as she sat brokenly in jail.

"You were supposed to *defend* her, Lawrence. Instead, you shattered her. You left her to fend for herself and you left her to figure out a problem that she should've *never* had. She was fifteen-years-old. She was *fifteen*," I nearly yelled. "You hugged your wife close as Sadie rode away in a police car, and you pretended to be astonished at the thought of her killing her baby. The reality of the situation is that you found the shoebox in your own closet. You cut the umbilical cord for her with the same scissors she used to cut her bangs. *You* found the shovel, and Lawrence? *You* dug the hole for her.

"I often think of what would've happened to Sadie if you *hadn't* been sneaking into her room every single night, Lawrence. Where would she be now? Would she be a doctor? An attorney? A teacher? What great things would she have accomplished if you were a father instead of a monster?

"Today, I am asking Judge Heany to give you the maximum sentence under Ohio law. I'm asking that he hand down a sentence that is befitting a monster because that is exactly what you are, Lawrence Traverty. You are a rapist, and you are a murderer. And I will spend the *rest* of my life ensuring that the mistakes that you made and the ripples that you've created no longer hurt other people. I will dedicate the *rest* of my life to helping girls just like Sadie.

"She had no one, Lawrence. And now? You have no one. I hope you wake up every single day with hope in your heart. I hope you wake up every single day with love in your heart. I hope you wake up every day optimistic. And then I hope the memory of what you have done crashes down on you like the waves in the Pacific. Every single day, I hope you get pummeled again and again with the knowledge that you wrecked the lives of the people that loved you more than anything.

"And when you go to bed at night? On a cot in a prison that is actually too good for you? I hope what you'll face one day in hell hangs over your head like a torturous cloud of agony. I hope you fall asleep every single night knowing that you are one day closer to your reckoning." I took a deep, deep breath. I raised my eyes to Lawrence Traverty for the very last time. "And I hope you dream about shoeboxes."

Tears flooded my eyes as I stepped back from the podium. I closed the folder in front of me. "Thank you," I said to the judge and he nodded back to me. My heels pounded on the wooden floor of the courtroom and the sound was loud in my ears. I sat back down on the bench and Elijah's hand fell around my shoulder.

"I will never stop being proud of you," he whispered. And that truth washed over me like the sun after a hurricane.

Endings are kind of funny, I think. Was the trial the end of my story? No. Was it the beginning? I don't think that's true, either. It was more of a rebirth. I walked out of that courtroom with a sense of purpose that I had never felt before. I walked out of that courtroom and the weight of the past six months pressed down on my shoulders.

I walked out of that courtroom knowing that nothing would ever be the same, but ... given the choice? I don't think I would've walked back to the person I was before.

Even if you offered me a billion dollars.

## Ending

**Epilogue: A final or concluding act or event**

*Six years later*

We named her Bridget because apparently, it meant goddess of fire and poetry. And all those years ago, I felt so strongly that she had been forged right in the middle of flames. Six years later, she is ... fiery.

She's also the light of our lives, and tonight, she's got her first role ever as an angel in the Christmas program at church. I think her dad is going to combust with pride and love, and I might just cry through the entire thing.

Elijah is busy hunting for her halo - which she thinks might be in her playroom. I'm braiding her long, curly blonde hair. From where the blonde streaks in her untamable hair comes from - I have no idea.

"You think next year they're going to let me be Mary?" She's got a doll in her small hands and hear me out - sometimes, even just looking at her hands makes me cry.

"Maybe. You'll have to ask Miss Nicole. I think Mary has a lot of lines to memorize. You think you can do that?" I pinned her braids up and off of her shoulders, and sent a quick prayer up that Eli could find the errant halo.

"Mommy," she turned and regarded me so seriously for her six years. "I'll be seven then. It'll be fine." She kissed my cheeks and hopped off of the barstool. "I think daddy needs my help."

Her Christmas dress swooshed around her knees and her polished black shoes click-clacked on the tile of the kitchen. I looked out the windows and out over to a sparkling, cold Cincinnati. This would be the last Christmas together in this apartment. Our house in the country would be finished later this spring, and we'd move.

I walked over to the windows and watched my breath fog in front of me. So many mornings, Eli had made pancakes at the stove. So many evenings, we cuddled together as a warm little trio. Bridget had learned to walk in this living room, and so many times - this tall, tall tower had felt like a fortress for us. A hideout.

"A-HA!" I heard from the hallway. "I FOUND IT!" Bridget giggled.

Together, the pair emerged from her playroom, and I was unsurprised to see Eli wearing the halo. Six years later, and he still could take my dang breath away. His dress pants hugged him in all of the best places, and his navy sweater stretched perfectly over his chest. I smiled at them both. "Are we ready?"

Eli helped us both with our coats, and held our hands, and opened the door. Jonathan, the head of our security team, stood ready. "Nice halo, sir," he said, pressing the button for our elevator.

We sat in a packed church, waiting for the program to begin. My parents sat right behind us - just as they always were. My stomach was tied in knots. I couldn't help the nerves. Whenever Bridget wasn't with me, I always felt the separation clear down to the marrow in my bones. I worried about her constantly, even though I knew that her own security detail was standing right next to her. I was certain the feeling would never go away, and I was certain the uneasiness stemmed from those brutal three days all those years ago.

"It'll be okay," Eli whispered in my ears. "She'll be okay." I looked at him and nodded as the lights lowered.

It was a program like you've seen one hundred times. Joseph forgot some of his lines and Miss Nicole whispered them from the front row. Baby Jesus - really, truly a baby - cried and had to be replaced with someone's baby doll from the third row. And then, our angel appeared.

And I cried because that, I've decided, is exactly what moms are supposed to do.

We stood and clapped and Bridget curtsied in her white angel robe. "I want a hundred just like her," Elijah whispered in my ear. Tears had gathered in his eyes. "She's perfect."

I smiled back at him and thought of the presents under the tree. There was one special one with his name scrawled across the tag. I had taken a pregnancy test earlier in the day, and then quickly wrapped it while he was getting dressed.

Bridget came running down the church hallway - her halo bobbing with each step. Quickly following her were two burly men in suits. I suppose they meant to blend in, but you could pick them out of a crowded room easily. They were not there to watch the Christmas Program. They were there to make sure we were safe.

"You were REMARKABLE!" Eli caught her as she jumped into his arms.

"Did you see me?! I winked at you like you told me to!" She flung her arms out wide like she was flying.

"I saw it," I said, leaning up to kiss her cheek. "You did a wonderful job!"

She leaned over to hug my dad. "Did you see, Papa? I stood still and smiled and next year, mommy told me I can probably be Mary. Do you think I can be Mary, too?" She was very serious, and she waited patiently for his answer.

"Baby girl, I think you can be anything you want." He started carrying her out of the church. Her long legs stretched down to his knees. Soon, she'd be too big to carry. "You can be a teacher, or a doctor ..." His words trailed off and yes.

She was going to set the world on fire.

And we would be right beside her to see it.

## Acknowledgements

The acknowledgement page is always the best page to write. I always keep it until the end, you know? It's like a bow on a present, or a piece of cheesecake after the best meal ever.

First off, I want to thank you – my dedicated reader. This book has been clanging around in my head for eight years. I've started it and stopped it more times than I can count, and the fact that you're still here and reading means more to me than I can ever describe.

Super special shoutout to my editor Kristi Rawley from Periplus Editing. She's the very, very best. Not only does she tell it like it is, but she knows every comma, apostrophe, and hyphen rule there ever was. And she earns all the bonus points for being an Aggie.

There are many, many people that put their hand on my shoulder and helped me limp this book baby to the finish line. From my parents to my husband Craig, from my son to my very best friends Betsy, Allie, and Nikki – each one of them urged and listened and pushed and read and re-read and –

All of it just made me realize how lucky I am.

Truly.

For each and every single one of you.

xoxo, B.

**Facebook:** Rebecca Cooper, Author
**Instagram:** @rebeccacooperauthor

Made in the USA
Monee, IL
26 February 2022